SWEET TEMPTATION

P. A. THOMAS

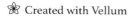

ABOUT SWEET TEMPTATION

I was Persephone claimed by Hades for thirty days. I wasn't watching where I was driving and slammed right into Ricardo Ruiz, the God of the Underworld.

He was a murderer.

Criminal.

I had no insurance.

No money.

And no way to pay for the repairs on his Aston Martin. I begged for a way to fix it off-record because. I couldn't afford another mark against me.

He told me hitting his car came at a price.

And the price was me.

Carcass by Agostino Venezianohas was painted on my ceiling. It reflected the evil in the world today, the cruelty of men and women against everyone they deemed to be beneath them. It symbolized my world, the darkness my family belonged to, and how we treated others. We used them, did cruel things to them to get whatever we wanted.

The walls had paintings by The Garden of Earthly Delights, a demonstration of our world today, even if it was painted in the fifteenth century. A world had succumbed to the temptations of evil and was reaping eternal damnation. The panel featured cold colors, and the nakedness of the human figures had nothing to do with erotica but highlighted the temptations man seeks. The darkness in this room was a reflection of the man who resided within it. The man who bathed naked in the bathroom and slept in this bed.

I had never seen goodness in anyone and knew I would fail to do so in the future. I closed my eyes, thinking about who will have to be killed or taught a lesson tomorrow. For now, all I could do was feel the effects of Louis XIII, my favorite liquor was taking its tow on my body. Tomorrow would be another day, not a brighter one, just another one filled with darkness.

I woke up, and it was still dark; after all, it was only five am. I had a strict schedule of waking up at the same time every day. In general, I didn't sleep much, maybe four to five hours at the most. I headed into the shower, and I didn't even bother to close the door. Only my housekeeper Lourdes lived with me, the rest of the staff start at seven. I tried not to be in the house while they were around; I couldn't stand people cleaning around me. It fucking irritated me.

I ran the cold water, feeling the need for a pick-up. Maybe I took too much of a shot last night, but I feel a little hungover, which is a surprise because I never drink to the stage where I was drunk. Then again, I did go out for a celebration with the gang last night. We had something to be happy about, so maybe this was why I felt like shit. When I looked down, I was still fully dressed.

What the fuck?

Something must have happened because the last thing I remembered was coming up to my room after talking to dad, and I was pretty sure, I was fucking naked; when did I get up to put clothes on?

No one would come in here, so I must be confused about how the night ended or something. Then it dawned on me; I needed to get my drinking under control. Lately, I've been waking up and not remembering things clearly. Thinking something like this happened when it fucking didn't.

Maybe I needed a special friend like dad advised me to do. I wasn't like him. I didn't use sex as a weapon, and I never felt delighted unless there was some connection with a woman. Fucking just for fucking's sake, it didn't work with me. The guys in our business functioned that way, but for me, it was the one thing I could never just think about regularly doing. My cousin Diego sometimes fucks three or four girls a night, but he's young. "It's all about pleasure, primo!" He would wink at me; if we're at his place or someone else's and a party is going on, he wouldn't hesitate in picking up a girl or two.

Life's too short; I've heard this repeated by so many different guys time and time again.

Maybe finding a woman should be my next move. Go out there and get someone, someone who's not in the business. Fuck, those women are so damn demanding, always wanting this and that.

A Mexican girl would be good for the first few months; then she would mingle, and before I knew it, she would be demanding. No, I needed someone to keep me company in the bedroom when or if I needed it.

Dad told me once he knew how to get someone for my needs. I would talk to him about it in the meeting; I had to get going for now. I was not too fond of tardiness and had to get there on time. Even if no one respected punctuality in my family, I did with all the passion in the world. I looked up at the antique clock that chimed in my bathroom. I had a fucking clock everywhere. Time was money; both things I couldn't afford to lose.

2

One week later...
Ricardo

IN THE ROOM at one of our hideouts, I sat alone, consumed with grief and anger. We didn't have many across the city, and we preferred them to be out of sight, but in Chicago, it was pretty hard to have hideouts in a city full of apartment blocks. So, we used one of the businesses we owned for cleaning money. The typical crap every mob king had, from restaurants to men's clothing stores. A casino could have been added to the list, but then the damn feds would be on it like leeches. We preferred restaurants because there was nothing more satisfying than beating the crap out of someone and then having a good meal afterward.

As much as I tried to erase the picture which kept flashing in my mind, I couldn't even if a whole week had passed by, it still felt like yesterday. No amount of food, time, or drink could ever get rid of it. I stood as if a shot of lightning was being directed at the chair. I recalled Pa's lifeless body lying in his bed. The man I loved more than myself was dead, and I didn't know or even care if I would ever feel the same way ever again.

Today marked one week.

One week since the day I lost him. I couldn't remember the last time someone in our family had died of natural causes; it was rarely heard of in our business, our lives were always fucking under threat. I'd sent many to their grave without blinking an eye. I'd had others try the same thing on me, and didn't hesitate in repaying the favor.

Booze.

Sex.

Women.

These vices made everything we did bearable, as we played Russian roulette with our lives; it was clear we would cross the line one day and miss. The day I found Pa dead, it changed everything for me. I felt numb as I reflected on it as if I'd done every fucking day since then.

Could I have done something differently?

If I'd known something was up, then somewhere along the lines, I could have stopped it. The million-dollar question that must run through everyone's mind when they lose a loved one.

I was born with a gun in one hand and a bottle of tequilia in the other. My Mexican grandpa raised me and any time we snuck across the border into the States, it felt like a fucking luxury.

Now, it felt like a necessity, which didn't sit too well with me at the best of times. When Wall Street crashed, my family and the rest of them chipped in to save America's fucking economy. We weren't known as criminals then, but saviors.

When it suits them, we're criminals so much so that their president is talking about building a damn wall to divide us. They should build the fucking wall and see how long they last without our *suicio dinero*. Our money's so fucking dirty when they need it to help them survive the economic crisis banging on their doors. The politicians and even bankers come and beg us for dough; they're interested in keeping us in the country, but the rest of the time, they treat us like we're animals. As if we're the ones who should be locked up in cages and thrown into the ocean.

Pa always said we had to scratch their backs because one day, they'd scratch ours. It was a fucking joke because, at times, it felt as if they were scratching ours and leaving fucking scars.

There was no break-in to the house, no sign anything was up, apart from one little detail. Pa wasn't up at six. Sometimes, he got up a little later...six-ten or so...but by six-thirty, I gathered something was up.

So, I went in to check on him. I knocked on his door. Nothing. "Pa! Llevantarte!" I laughed as I thought about him having a little too much to drink, and needing a little sunlight to come into the room. This would wake him up for sure, I thought as I drew the curtains. My eyes glanced back, and he was peacefully sleeping in his bed. Or so I believed...

It wasn't until, I looked at him closely, while he was sleeping in his bed. I froze, not wanting to disturb him. But something looked off. He was so still and pale, unlike his usual tanned complexion, so I leaned closer to him, intending to kiss his forehead. His skin was cold. I gasped, rocking back on my heels.

He wasn't breathing.

I threw back the covers, but they stuck to his body.

Gagging, I stumbled backward. Someone had carved him up like a fucking butcher.

My Pa.

The paramedics and police turned up; they were too late. The fucking pigs laughed, and I even overheard them, saying someone saved a few thousand people by killing Pa.

What few thousand people?

We killed, sure, but they were killing innocents, politicians putting families on the poverty line, but we were the animals. And no one's innocent in this world.

No one.

I told them to put Pa in the fridge. He wouldn't be buried, and he couldn't be put to rest until I found out who killed him. I would put everything to the side. Nothing was important than seeing justice served.

Juan, my right-hand man, a former boxer, walked into the room and said, "Listo, jefe." His eyes were dark, and he had no hair. He shaved it a long time ago when he started to go bald. It made him appear a lot younger than his years.

"It's time, Juan. Time to learn what the mark knows."

Juan narrowed his eyes and nodded, in agreement.

"Someone, somewhere, knows who did this to Pa, and I won't rest until I find them." No fucking sleeping, eating, or anything which could be deemed as a luxury. I could still feel Pa's cold body against mine. Someone did this to him. Forensics said most of it was done when he was alive. I'd make whoever did it pay, and anyone involved suffer the same fate."

I sprung up with a spurge of energy, ready to beat the shit out of the mark. "Let's see what he knows."

Juan nodded, and I deliberated about the number of times I'd done this in my life. The figure was nowhere how many times I'd done it this week already. I stopped counting after the fifth. I needed to find Pa's killer, and most of all, I needed to make them pay.

3

Veronica

AT MY DESK, uncomfortable as always, I tried to maneuver and find a way for my pencil skirt not to cling to every part of my body so I could respire properly. I was fine standing up, but I felt as if someone had a tight rope across my stomach the moment I sat down. I decided to look around to make sure no one was watching, so I could undo my button at the back and breathe without feeling as if I was suffocating. I sighed as my zipper naturally opened as I sat up a bit, and my stomach hung over my skirt.

I closed my eyes, wondering why I kept punishing myself like this. I hadn't put on a little weight, but a lot of weight, and the refusal to buy new clothes wasn't an option anymore. This was the only skirt I could fit in this morning; as for the shirt, luckily it didn't have buttons and stretched over my breasts. As for the matching suit-jacket, it couldn't close. I didn't need to close it anyway; I could walk around the office with it open, unlike my winter jacket, which I would wear for only a few moments outside before jumping in a taxi.

I didn't see Gold's secretary walking to my desk; I was too busy thinking about whether to go to a store. Any store nearby and find something to fit. Anything. Today was going to be a long day, and it would be even longer if I didn't get something I could breathe in because come lunchtime, I wouldn't be able to eat.

"Veronica, he wants to see you in his office," she purred as her long pink fingernail stroked along the surface of my desk. She got to the end and lifted her finger as if to check for dust on my desk, and I rolled my eyes. Her very presence annoyed me, and her petty actions just wound me up even more.

I was about to get fired. It was a known trait in my office when the big boss called you not by putting an appointment in your calendar or even sending an email. When he sent his little Chihuahua (our nickname for his secretary) to come and get you, it wasn't good news. Her blonde hair was in a perfect bun, and her square-clear glasses, which she didn't need (a rumor which I wasn't sure if it was true because I'd seen her wear it in the office, but never outside.) Her glasses hung on her square-nose a little too far. Her blue eyes lit up as she stood with her arms crossed, ready for me to follow her. I felt like a lamb being led to be slaughtered.

Hank Gold resided on the top floor; he was old money, his father and father passed on the business before him. He made it known he was money, so important, he resided on the twenty-foot !!!! building's top floor. No one could go up there apart from him and his Chihuahua, who smiled at me with her sea-blue eyes. This was the reason why after one year of working here we'd given her name because Mr. Gold treated her as if she was more precious than anyone else who worked in this office, and she loved to flaunt it. She enjoyed being followed up to the top floor; it was as if she got a kick out of having the power to see us go.

Well, she didn't have the authority to do it, but she made us feel small as if she had us at the palm of her hand.

"Mr. Gold doesn't like to be kept waiting," she commanded as she faced me and put her finger once again on my desk. I hated everything about Mr. Gold, from the way he sat in his high tower to how he commanded his little pet to come and fetch us. Mr. Gold was a married man, and everyone knew he was fucking her; she didn't even try to hide it. We knew if Mrs. Gold found out, it would cost him a lot more than this tower.

I counted to three as I tried to squeeze my legs together and pulled down my pencil length skirt. It was too tight; who would have thought one week of binge eating and drinking would struggle to zip this up without lying down first. I stood up straight as I held on to the little pride I had left. She looked at me strangely, as if we were friends and I'd done something out of the ordinary.

The only thing I did was smile at her, showing all my teeth, which wasn't a good idea because I needed to go to the dentist to get my teeth whitened, the hairstylist to get rid of my split ends, and more importantly, the optician to get new contacts. The last one would have to wait; I knew if I got new contacts, everyone would know the green eyes I claimed to be natural were actually contacts.

I pulled my jacket from behind my chair, but no more quick movements in case my skirt split at the seams. Thank goodness I was wearing a blouse and not a shirt today; otherwise, it would be soaking wet from overheating because it would be clutched to my skin, and my buttons would be popping right now. I didn't feel well. Not one little bit.

Jen, my bestie and only work friend, smiled at me. The kind of smile told me she was rooting for me. But we both knew this moment was coming from last week. The week I spent all night working on the presentation for not one client but two and ended up completely fucking it up. One year of complete loyalty and doing more than my call of duty should have made a difference, but it didn't. I received an email from him saying he would call me when he was ready, and from the look in the Chihuahua's eye, I could tell he was more than ready.

I walked past my desk empty-handed, knowing I would need nothing but my pride as I headed towards the elevator. I could hear the whispers. The lack of subtlety in the office was unreal, as others pretended to need to go somewhere, anywhere to tell another what was going on. I was not too fond of the uncertainty and wished I had never signed up for this job. The ad said Marketing Executive when it should have said Slave to The Gold God. I'd done more than marketing since I joined, and when I compared it to a couple of my friends in the same field, they'd said it wasn't a Management role I was doing, but more of an Executive role on a Management salary. I didn't complain, no I didn't even raise my voice at the idea of it because I knew once I had a couple of years' experience here, I could go wherever I wanted, and they would say, "You put up with Gold, you need a medal." The staff turnover here was too high, and Gold didn't care, all he wanted was results, and he got them.

Carrie, his secretary, had worked here the longest, five years out of all of us, and we all knew the reason for it was her extra activities upstairs.

I took a deep breath as I considered my fate as the elevator doors opened. It was a now or never type moment, and part of me wished it'd be never, but it wasn't an option I had control of, not at the moment.

Carrie walked in with her five-inch heels and pressed the button to go upstairs, and she was about to put her card in when she snapped, "You coming in or not?"

I nodded as all the nerves started to take over my body.

"Is he there alone?"

She shook her head. "No. HR is waiting in my room. He wants to speak to you alone before letting them speak to you."

She gave me a strange look as if she was thinking the same thing I did. Usually, everything would be done simultaneously, but I had a feeling it wouldn't be the case this time, and it gave me something I didn't think was possible: hope. I didn't have a chance of staying here, but I had exactly eleven months left to get the dreams I had envisaged from the moment I started here, and I wasn't willing to give up on those.

Not yet.

It put a smile on my face; I could see Carrie saw it and spun her head around as if to check my reflection was real. Somehow, it put a frown on hers, and I realized she was a bitch through and through. The type who only thought of their own happiness and no one else's. I didn't have a bone in my body to ever hate someone; it wasn't in me. I wouldn't say I liked Carrie. She reminded me not every woman had the same sense of responsibility in the workplace. We wanted to unite, but women like her didn't care as long as they got what they wanted.

The doors swung open, and she strode out slowly into the glass hallway. I'd only been up here once, and even then, no one gave me a tour. Mr. Gold congratulated me for doing a top job with a couple of clients. The account should have only been fifty thousand, and somehow, I'd managed to get them to spend nearly a quarter of a million. I was talented, I knew, but I didn't realize how much until I sealed the deal with the account. I celebrated not only bringing in the additional clients, but the ten grand bonus that came with it.

I smiled, the cool air circulating around my body as I moved behind her. She was in control of her movement, whereas I always felt like my steps would break the glass floor one day. Crazy, I know, but I wasn't used to walking on glass, unlike

Carrie who strutted with her stilettoes as if she owned the place as if she had the power to make the glass break if she wanted to.

I lightly lifted my feet as I walked, which was pretty hard to do when the damn skirt was so tight. Every movement I made, made me feel uncomfortable as I spent more time trying to keep up with her and less on where we were going. The doors slid open, and I knew meant one thing, we'd arrived at his office.

"Ms. Smith is here."

"Good, send her in."

Technically, I was already in because as the doors slid open I had followed Carrie into the office.

Once again she smiled, nodding. He wasn't sitting at his desk, but on the white sofa at the back of his office.

Maybe it wasn't all bad news; maybe there was some hope.

4

R icardo

FUCK!

My knuckles cracked against his face. I'd told myself the only boxing I would do these days would be against a punching bag. I would change my ways and stop fucking hurting people.

Six months ago, I'd had a widow turn up at my door with her child, claiming I'd killed her husband. I told her I didn't do it, but what I didn't tell her was I had ordered the hit on him.

She was better off without him. The man had a woman in nearly every state and most likely more children, but it wasn't my business to dig into her love life. No, I wasn't any marriage counselor, for sure. But I did make a promise after seeing her son's blue eyes swell with tears as his mom said, "This is the man who killed your father."

I promised to stop being the monster I'd been for so long, and try and value the life in front of me, unless I really had to put it to an end. Just like a leopard couldn't change it's spots, I knew that I was kidding myself by making such a promise.

I knew even if he was a shit husband, he was a dad. I'd been paying all their living expenses since the day that had happened, but finding Pa dead made me break the promise I made all those months ago. Everything had gone through the fucking window.

What mob king didn't inflict violence on another?

None.

I was fucking kidding myself if I thought I could stay in this line of work and not inflict harm on others. It went with the job description, the one dad had told me from the start. We lived by violence, and we died by it. I had to get revenge on whoever killed the old man, no doubt, like me, he most likely deserved it.

"You going to talk, or you want me to do some real damage?"

Fuck, I sounded so old-fashioned, like I was in my sixties and not my forties. Pa was my only living parent. My mom died by a slit to the throat when I was five. It took dad two days to figure out who did it and exact revenge not only on the man himself but his whole family. He wiped out a whole bloodline when mom died. Dad had been dead a whole fucking week and so far, all I'd hit were dead walls. It made me want to take out my gun and pop Mario. There was no fucking way no one knew nothing.

Impossible. Someone knew. The issue was, no one was talking.

"Ricardo, think about mi mama, she'll be alone if you do this," Mario whimpered as I held his throat in one hand, his dark strands wet from sweat and fear thinking I was going to kill him. His dark eyes were half-closed, one eye because Juan had thumped him as soon as we took him. The other eye could barely manage to stay open. I had my gun in my other hand, just in case I got fed up and decided to pop him.

Sometimes, this was the problem with these interrogations. I wouldn't get the answer I needed, and I would pop the mark by accident due to impatience. I didn't want to do with Mario. I knew Ma, Mario's mom was powerful, and if I crossed the line, which I was already doing, it would end in a turf war. I wanted to know who did the hit on dad and be done. This fucking game of someone does a hit on you; they tread on your toes, so you do the same on them the classic cat and mouse, was tired and old.

Having the control and power to do whatever I wanted all the time, was a dream come true. Until I got older and lost friends, close friends were part of the circuit; they'd died. Always a horrible death and then the same thing would happen, like what was happening now, it was a vicious circle and him talking about his mom wasn't helping.

"How many people has Ma knocked off?"

He blinked a little too long for me to believe he didn't fucking know. He must have been blind, deaf, or dumb not to realize his mom ran the Northside, not his uncle. Everyone knew his Ma was the balls of the family, but to her sweet innocent son, she was his Ma. Everyone called her Ma for a reason, and it had nothing to do with her skills in the kitchen but more to do with her organizational skills. The idea of him not knowing made me want to stop doing what my gut instinct was telling me to do.

And that was to take him out.

"None. Ma cooks and nothing else. She's my Ma..." he was sniffing and crying like a baby. Not so much because of the possibility I was going to take him out, but because he was completely innocent.

Mario knew nothing; he didn't even know his Ma was the Queen on East side. No, he needed to be saved; I could tell him what he didn't know and use him. Shit, everyone used someone, especially in this business, and I intended to do it now and use it to my fucking advantage.

I FELT as if I was at peace, but I could see the horror on Mario's face as I told him about his mom. All the hits his uncle had done had been in the palm of his Ma's hand. They were nothing but puppets on a string. The woman was ruthless; one time I could have sworn Pa was a little scared of her, and he walked around as if fear was his number one enemy, and he didn't possess it at all or even have it in his vocabulary.

"I don't believe it. She's my Ma. She gave birth to me; she wouldn't."

I took off the rope that was around his legs to stop him running off, and sat opposite him, and talked to him man-to-man, I left out the gory details, not all of them, but the list was too fucking long of the number of people she'd taken out. There was one particular person I knew would be of interest to him. The love he lost, and the reason why.

The guy was hurting; he'd been living a lie. Sure, he was young and had been protected from being involved in taking people out, but he was still involved in some ways, even if he pretended he didn't know what went on behind closed doors.

Sunday lunches Ma invited the main guys over to talk business. And anyone she wanted rid of, she made them a special plate. So special she would put it in a tub for them to take home and made sure they never got home to eat it. Whoever left with a tub in their hand had been given their last supper. It was the sign for her men to take a hit on them.

Shit, when she found out Mario was gay, his piano teacher had been giving him two types of lessons, the teacher met his death not by his uncle's hand, but by Ma's. She did that one personally; she didn't want anyone to have the pleasure of taking him out. She made him suffer, so Pa told me. But I spared Mario those details. I knew he was hurting enough, I didn't have to rub salt on his wound.

Mario was crying like a baby because he believed his Ma had accepted him. She did, as long as he never slept with another man in his life. She made sure the word got out, no gay bar, club, or any kind would let Mario get in. He was young now, but he would have figured it out later, his Ma wasn't the innocent one in the family. He'd spent so many years trying to figure out how to come out and deal with his sexuality maybe he'd turned a blind eye to the truth behind his family and like Pandora's box, I'd opened it up for him.

"Ricardo, tell me it's not true. I loved him."

No more did I have him bound up with a gun to his head; he'd suffered a loss like I had. A love so deep no one could replace it.

"Mario, listen to me. I need your help. I need to figure out who killed my dad. I need this shit to stop."

He was distressed and tired as I cut him loose. The rope around his body was loosened, the ones that tied his hands behind his back were cut. He used his free hands to simultaneously wipe his eyes and the blood, which was pouring down his forehead from the beating I'd given him earlier.

"What do you need from me?" he said as if he had a surge of energy. Anger had taken over where fear once was.

"I need you to be in the house with your eyes wide open, and your ears sharp, after you tell her that you're away for a few days. So, she doesn't see the mess I made to your face. Besides you'll need time to heal maybe a week or two."

He knew what to do, he'd been on the lookout for his uncle a couple of times and they said he was good when you gave him something to focus on. If you told him to do a job, and be present, he would be present.

She hated her son being gay; she'd voiced it many times behind his back, it was a case of everyone knew—everyone apart from Mario. The poor kid believed his ma had accepted him, but deep down she hated everything 'his kind' represented, which I thought was ironic.

They'd never killed or caused any harm to anyone, not like our kind; we fucking killed in the flash of an eye, yet Ma felt as if we should be accepted by society and her loving son shouldn't be.

I couldn't deal with all this shit. I needed to focus, and find out who killed my dad and then take revenge, even if it meant it would be the last time I would be alive. It was a risk I was willing to take. I'd never known anything other than the life I'd been brought up to lead and I didn't know any better. Or rather I didn't want to. I hated the idea of using Mario as a pawn because if it all went sour, then he would be the one to suffer for it. Besides there wasn't anything Ma didn't know; she was sure to know something..

"I'll make her pay for what she's done."

I nodded and signaled for Juan to set him free. I had to get the clean shirt out of the back of my car, look half-decent and get across town to repeat the same thing all over again. This time, I wasn't sure if I would be so willing to let him go. I had so much frustration built up inside of me, one for thinking Mario knew his Ma was a monster, and then the other for knowing I'd turned him against her.

It should have made me feel better, knowing I would get the results I'd been trying to get every day during this week.

Nothing made me feel good, though.

Nothing.

5

V eronica

"VERONICA, SIT. CARRIE, YOU CAN GO," Mr. Gold demanded as he stood. He didn't try to stall what was about to happen next. I looked around his ice-cold office, thinking maybe HR would pop up from somewhere, anywhere. But they didn't. For now, we were alone as the sliding doors closed. Carrie left with a big smile on her face; no doubt she would reward him for getting rid of me.

"Veronica, I'm not going to beat around the bush. You know why you're here?" He said as he slowly moved towards me, pointing at the sofa as if to tell me to sit.

He didn't come next to me straight away, but pressed a button and then out of the wall, a bar magically appeared. Had he watched some video on minimalism? Then decided the only way to have an office as cold as possible, was to make every-thing was in it appear from nowhere. Hidden, so no one could know what was truly in the office. I started to wonder if the sofa was hidden, and he pressed a button to make it appear. My mind started wandering as I looked around, trying to find any other hidden buttons. I only did this type of thing when I was nervous; I would start looking for something, anything to focus on rather than the matter at hand.

He handed me a glass, no doubt it was Hennessy Paradis Imperial, apparently his favorite drink. I'd heard some of the guys say it cost more than some of us make in a week. What's the point of such luxuries? Once a drink goes down, you'll end up pissing it out. It's not like you could savor it. Not like a good meal; then again, this must be the joys of being rich, I suppose. Something I've never had and a life I don't think I'll ever get accustomed to living.

I grabbed it with both hands as I uncomfortably sat at the end of the sofa.

"You can move down the sofa, I'm not going to bite."

I looked up at his dark eyes as he never made an appearance downstairs for the first time in a while; he'd lost a lot of weight, not a pound or two; but stones. Loads of it. I wondered if he had been sick, and this was his road to recovery. He looked completely different, not the middle-aged man, but an athletic man with a few lines and crop type blond hairs with a square jawline. What a difference weight-loss can make to a person, he appeared to be someone completely different.

I didn't say anything, as my eyes deliberated about the very expensive Hennessy Paradis which was in my hand; I smelled it discretely, and then took a sip. There was no sharp taste; if anything, it was warm and pleasant.

He sat down next to me, a little too close, and asked, "What do you think?"

I summed it up in one word, "Nice."

He smiled, jerked his head back, and emptied his once quarter-filled shot glass. I did the same, but it made me cough.

As I regained my composure he said nothing as he smiled. A smile I didn't like and didn't expect from him. A smile made my heart beat as he drew closer to me, like a moth to a flame.

"Do you want some more?" I nodded, as his breath was so close, no more was I smelling the cognac I'd downed, but everything he'd eaten today.

"You know what today's about? You cost the company money and there's a price for it."

He magically took the cup out of my hand, and then he placed it to my side, and moved even closer. I moved away from him; I knew if he moved any closer he'd be sitting on my damn knee.

But he followed suit until there wasn't any couch left, and I knew there was only one thing to do.

Leave.

I was about to do when he put his hand on my knee and growled, "I could make all of this go away. If you agree to some new terms."

I was tempted, the old Mr. Gold, hell no. But the new one was sexy as hell. I hadn't paid the insurance on my car and rent was getting more expensive. His hands were moving up my thighs, his lips were getting closer, and I hadn't even heard the terms yet.

"Mr. Gold, I'm not that type of girl," I shot up at the realization he wanted me to prostitute myself. The problem was I hadn't been raised like that. This kind of thing was okay with some girls like Carrie, but not with me.

He laughed. "Everyone has their price, and you need this job. You need a new car, rent, and I don't even need to tell you all the other reasons you need to do this."

He'd struck a chord. He'd done his homework and decided I would be at his beck and call.

"I'm not desperate," I snapped as I moved away from him. I had to get to the sliding doors, figure out where the button was, and get the fuck out of here. I searched for the room like a madwoman, trying to walk quickly and get as far away from Mr. Gold as possible.

"Stop playing hard to get, it's boring. You know leaving here means no one will hire you. No one. They send your debt to the collection, and before you know it, you'll be living on the street," he said as he faked a yawn.

I shot a glance at him, seeing he was sitting on the sofa, with his legs crossed, and I hated him even more for summing my fate up in one sentence, with it ending with me needing to suck his cock or some other sexual act to stop it happening the way he was describing it.

"You need this job. You know it and I know it. The question is, are you willing to do what it takes to keep it."

I didn't hesitate as I blurted out, "No. Fuck you and your precious job. I'll get another one."

Great, I figured out where the door was and there was no one, and nothing was going to stop me from going through with it. I strode to it with all the confidence and I started to walk through it.

He shouted, "You'll be back."

I shook my head saying, "No. I fucking won't."

As I went through the door, nerves started to take over me, but I didn't care, I just kept walking.

I ignored HR and Carrie as they called out to me after I passed her office.

"Veronica, I am calling you. Stop walking away from me!" Carrie screamed out, and I realized I wasn't scared about walking on glass anymore. Somehow it'd become the least of my problems and I needed to get out of this fucking building and as far away from him as possible.

I turned around to face her.

"What?"

She looked bemused as she ran a couple more steps to get next to me.

"Why are you leaving? Didn't he offer you a way out?"

Shit, she knew!

"What is wrong with you? You know how he operates and you stay by him."

She shook her head, "His wife stands by him. I get what I can. This is the real world, honey!"

I chuckled. "Not my world."

She snarled, reducing the distance between us, "Well, let's see how far you get sitting on your high horse. You seen Linda lately? She left here, still can't get a job. She's back home with her family in Minnesota. Don't be naïve; this is a man's game. You need to play their game and then when you're ready, leave. Don't let them have the upper hand, you have it all the time."

"I'm not giving away my body to keep a job."

She backed away from me and said, "Well, it doesn't look as if you think so much about your body, so I don't get why you're so scared about it."

I slapped her, without hesitation, and the shock of it all was written all over her face as she grabbed her face as if it was a precious stone. I didn't wait around for her to hit back. I kept on walking, and as if on cue, the elevator doors opened and I stepped in. I didn't have to press the floor, it did it automatically. I would have to call Jen to meet me downstairs with my purse and phone. I had left them at my desk. The elevator took me to the ground floor, when his voice over the speaker.

"You don't have to worry about getting your things. They're downstairs in the parking garage. You have two days to think about my offer, or it'll no longer be on the table."

I stuck two fingers up in the air, knowing somewhere in here, there was a camera. I felt dirty and cheap, not only by his offer but Carrie's assessment of my body. They made me feel as if I was nobody as if I would do whatever and anything to stay in my position. As if I was desperate.

I didn't have to stay in this town. I knew somewhere, there would be someone who would make a difference in my life. It wasn't all bleak; I wasn't going to let it get to me. I'd worked two jobs to get through college, worked off my butt once I finished trying to pay these damn student loans and I wasn't going to let this job make me feel I was worth nothing.

No fucking way.

6

Ricardo

"BOSS, YOU TAKING YOUR CAR?" Juan asked as he put his thick fingers on the door handle. His questions were always direct, to the point, emotionless. Sometimes, I wondered if boxing had made him that way or something else.

"Yeah," I sighed, scratching my head. Normally, I would have him drive, sit at the back and cool down before facing my enemy. Today I needed to drive to clear my mind a little before my next encounter. He looked uncertain and I continued. "Don't worry about it. I'll be alright."

He hesitated and then his stutter appeared out of nowhere, which had started in his boxing days.

"O... ok!"

One doctor said he was hit in the head so fucking hard everything would be rusty for the next couple of years. Five years ago, he wanted the championship like his uncle, and had the physique for it. He towered over me at six foot five with his dark eyes and bald head, and had a way of scaring everyone who came into contact with him. I considered him to be a gentle giant deep down. Back then, he hated the mob life, he wanted nothing to do with it. Somehow kicking someone's ass in the ring and getting paid for it, with thousands of people cheering you, was more acceptable. I never understood the logic when it came to being part of the mob. Then again, it was all about tradition and loyalty. He didn't want to be part of it, but after being told he couldn't perform anymore, he ended up in it, anyway.

Nothing else.

"You looked pretty messed up in there. You sure you're all right?"

I was about to nod and lie when I realized there was no point in lying. We didn't talk much, not the kind of way two brothers or even cousins talked about their lives. There was no point in having those types of conversations, they were wasted energy. He could tell by my body language exactly how I was feeling; he just wanted confirmation.

"I miss him, and I feel useless about not finding out who took him away from me."

He sighed, "We all missed him. But you know you need some rest. Trying to catch the killer is tiring you out, jefe."

This hit had nothing to do with someone treading on our toes, but it had revenge written all over it. No one was talking because we were looking in all the wrong places. I remember asking Pa if after he wiped out the family which killed Ma, it made him feel better. His answer was clear. "No. It won't bring her back."

Finding out the truth wasn't going to bring Pa back but it would make me feel a lot better. The smug look on the detective's face when he showed up at the scene, made me feel sick. Pa was in bed, but underneath the covers, he'd been butchered. The coroner said he'd been alive for the best part of it.

Someone had wanted to torture Pa, and I pondered as I put the key in to start the car, if it was one of the many broken hearts he'd created over the years. Pa wasn't good at relationships, especially after Ma. Juan begged me at one point to tell him to hire a girl. Have her and make her fulfill his every need, I talked to Pa about it, he wouldn't have it. In some fucked up way, he wanted them to suffer the pain he had due to Ma not being around, and I wondered if one of them had decided to do the same to him. They wanted to teach him the meaning of pain. I nodded to Juan as I spun the car out of the car park. I didn't know if he could see me, but I hated my thoughts even nearly as much as I hated everyone right now.

7

eronica

I SHUFFLED THROUGH MY BACK, which had been neatly waiting on a trolley and walked out of the elevator when it opened a moment later. I couldn't believe my purse was there; someone could have taken it. Then again, there were cameras everywhere in this damn place. I sighed as I grabbed it, thinking I'd call Jen and tell her to meet me for lunch.

No phone.

Shit, of course!

It was the company phone. I had gotten rid of my personal line trying to cut back on bills. It felt silly having a private phone when I could use work's. Now, not only had I lost a cell, but all my numbers. Jen told me to back up my numbers from the time I cut my line, but I didn't listen and the only number I knew by heart was hers.

My pass wasn't working as I got to the security gate to leave the building in my car, I considered embarrassing myself and telling security I'd been fired. I needed to get out of the building. Mr. Precious Gold had thought of everything else; why didn't he let my pass work so I could leave? He'd fucking done it on purpose, which just made me even madder. I had to press the intercom and explain it to security and get the fuck out of here.

"Hey."

"Veronica is that you?"

Fred Martin was on the other line, a security guard, who'd had a crush on me from the first time I met him in the lobby. I felt sorry for him; he was sweet, kind, and cute in his own little way. A little too skinny for me, but he had sparkling blue eyes, which hid behind his framed-glasses, and he was a good guy. The type of guy would treat me right on a date, open the car door, come to pick me up, and agree with everything I said on the date.

He was too good for me.

He was the kind I could take home to meet my mom if she was still around and they would be instantly happy I'd found someone decent. Yeah, he deserved someone who would appreciate him for his good heart, and I knew I wasn't that type of girl, I would be bored in an instant. He deserved better. It wouldn't be right to lead him on, so I rejected every date he offered even as tempted as I was to go on a couple of them. Jen said I was too hard on him, and even harder on myself. She felt the reason I rejected him more than a few times wasn't because he was a good guy, but simply because I believed I didn't deserve someone so great subconsciously. Maybe she had a point. Mr. Gold had pointed out I didn't deserve anyone decent, it'd been in my head before the words came out of his mouth.

"Veronica?" he asked again.

I shook my head, thinking about the nightmare I'd put myself into. I was standing by the intercom, as I did every morning to get into the building, and every night to get out. I couldn't use my pass from my car because the windows weren't working. I had to physically get out of the car from the passenger side. The driver side was okay to open, but a bitch to close. Yep, my car was beaten up, but it took me from home to work, so the little extras such as a door that worked, heating during winter, and A/C during the summer just felt like luxuries. Ones I couldn't afford to pay. I could use public transport, but with the hours I worked, I didn't feel safe getting on the metro at that time of night.

"Yes. It's me. I've..."

He sighed, "I know. I'll let you out. I suppose I'll have no one else to ask on a date anymore."

Even now, he was sweet. Over one year of trying and he still had it in his mind that I would cave one day. I laughed, "And you'll have no one telling you a raincheck. But hey, you know the next time you ask, I may not say raincheck."

The bar went up, and I ran to the passenger side of the car, closed the door, then I slid over to the driver's side. I'd been doing it for so long, it came naturally.

He called out my name as I drove my car through, I smiled about telling Jen tonight about my new number and letting her pass it on. There was some positive in all this, I couldn't let go of my pride. I couldn't let the tears falling uncontrollably, get to me. I had to put them aside, this was a new adventure.

Who was I kidding?

I was broke, penniless, overweight, and borderline ready to prostitute myself. I had to get out of this building as fast as possible, and far away from here.

8

R icardo

I COULDN'T GO THERE DIRECTLY, and not with so much fucking emotion running through my head. I couldn't appear frail, not in this fucking business. I had to make a pit stop at home. It was the other side of town, but I didn't give a fuck, they could wait. A quick shower and a change of clothes would set me straight. Right now, I was so fucking emotional. I still had Mario's tears and cries running through my ears as if he was in the car with me. He'd stopped the moment I told him what his mom had done, when anger took over him. I couldn't regret what I'd done; no, I couldn't cave.

My phone rang so I turned it off. I didn't even feel like listening to the radio. What I needed was a shot of whiskey, the smoke of a cigar, and a shower and a change; then I'd be back to normal.

"What the fuck!"

I screamed out as the lights turned red and I did an unnatural stop. Someone was testing my patience today. My car jumped the lane as the car behind me bashed into me, and I swung the door open to see who had smashed into the back of my car.

My Aston Martin Valkyrie had hardly any damage, but her car was a mess, but then, I had a feeling it had been beaten up before it smashed into me. She sat in her car, trying to get past the airbag and waving her hand up in the air.

"Shit!" I screamed out, seeing the smoke coming out of it. I shouted to her, "Get the fuck out of there!"

I didn't know why she was sitting there, until I realized she couldn't get the door open. I had an ax at the front of my car. I lifted the hood, got out the ax.

"Get back," I said, then smashed the ax against the window and reached inside to yank the door open. It swung open before it dropped on the ground like a ton of bricks. I quickly moved out of the way, worried her car was about to explode. Given the choice of me using an ax and her car having so much fucking smoke come out of it; she remained in her car, coughing. I didn't know what scared her more, me with the ax or her car.

I gave her a hand because she was struggling to get out of the car. It was as if her butt was glued to the seat as she stretched out past the airbag.

"Help!" she whimpered, but my other hand still had the ax in it and I dropped it to the ground as I moved towards her, as she tried to get up.

"Thank you," she said and then I started to get paranoid; was this an accident or did she do it on purpose?

"Who the fuck are you?" I growled, not caring who heard me, as onlookers looked at her car as we moved away from it. I asked if everyone was alright.

She shook her head. "Veronica Smith. Sorry, I hit your car. I thought you were going. I didn't think you would stop, and I didn't know the airbag was still working. Nothing else works in the damn car."

She was rambling, out of fear and probably confusion too.

"So, you rammed right into me. Where did you learn to drive?"

"Chicago."

I didn't expect her to answer, the fear in her eyes told me she was scared as I still held on to her. Her breasts were against my chest, the heat of her breath on my neck slowing down, but surely turning me on. I pushed her away from me.

I was going to ask her something else, but then a pig showed up, and I could tell by the way he looked at me, he knew exactly who I was, and he wanted to cause some trouble.

"Ma'am are you alright?"

She nodded, "I'm sorry, but I had a rough day and I wasn't paying attention."

It was then I noticed her skirt was falling apart at the seams. She was pretty, busty with emerald eyes and her hair looked as if it was partway tied up and lose. She wore a jacket and shirt which were tight; her formal attire told me she worked in one of the offices. The strange thing about it, she said she'd had a rough day. It was only eleven in the morning, how bad could her morning have been?

"Was this man harassing you in some way?" He cut his eyes at me, and then he was shocked as I moved to get my ax.

"Put the weapon down, Ricardo Ruiz."

I shook my head, "I was helping her get out of her car after she rammed into me."

I ignored him. What was he going to do? He appeared to be a rookie as his dark eyes shifted between her and me nervously and he adjusted his cap with one hand, while looking for his gun. He was feeling his waist, he fucking didn't know what he was doing because he seemed to know nothing about protocol. I picked up the ax, and walked away from him, not to him.

"Look, Ms. Smith. Give me your details. I'll talk to my insurance, you do the same with yours and we can sort it out," I said before the rookie did something he would fucking regret. One call was all it would take to not only take him out, but his entire fucking family.

She nodded, and then the rookie came up close to me, as I was about to get into my car, to get my card to give it to her.

"I don't know what was going on before I came, but you need to watch your step," he warned me as he followed me like a fucking dog.

I shook my head and said, "Rookie Price," as I read his badge. "You need to watch yours."

I still had the ax in my hand. So, I lifted the front, and this time, put it at the front of my car, the rookie decided to do his job and call for back-up and a tow. I could have stood and helped her out, but I needed to relax, before getting on with the job I had to do.

"Here's my details. My card. Call me or give this to your insurance company," I handed it to her, and she didn't say a word, as she just looked at it, and then her eyes bounced back to me, and the card again. I didn't know if she was in some state of shock or not, but I really had to get going, so I asked as I ran out of patience, "And yours?"

She ran to her car, and then nearly all the contents of her bag dropped out. She picked up a card, scratched out everything on it.

"I just lost my job. So, I have no phone. Here, this is my best friend. I'll write my plate, and full name, so you can contact me. I'll call you, the moment I have a phone," she babbled as I took her card. The rest of the information she had given me was pointless, but I didn't argue.

I didn't wait for the rookie to tell me it was ok for me to

leave. I hadn't done anything wrong. As soon as I got back inside my car, I decided I would check the damage properly when I got home.

I put in a call to Jose, an associate and part of my main team. He was Juan's twin brother. Unlike his brother, we spoke a lot more in general. He loved small talk, it didn't mean he was the friendly guy who would run around giving everyone besos, but the type that would greet and say bye, which was more than Juan did at the best of times. The light turned green, and I took a deep breath as I waited for Jose to pick up.

"Boss, what do you need?"

I gritted my teeth and said, "To teach a rookie called Price in District 32 a lesson."

He said, "I'm on it."

Then he hung up. The rookie made a mistake, one he would regret tonight and probably for the rest of his life. As for Veronica Smith, I would deal with her later. What had happened had, gotten her rattled, had her up close and personal to me, and I could still smell her flowery perfume on my shirt. She'd aroused me in a short space of time, I didn't even think I was alive down there, nothing had done that in a long time. Or rather no one.

9

eronica

I WAS SHAKING SO HARD I had to clench my teeth to keep them from chattering when they took my car, the smoke luckily having stopped coming out of it. I checked my account and I had exactly two hundred and fifty dollars to my name. It wouldn't last me long, but my rent wasn't due until next month, so I had a whole twenty-five days to come up with a new job.

My insurance had lapsed, but I could pay for a new policy, and then tell them about the accident. I shook my head at the idea which had lasted all of five seconds. It wouldn't work because I would have to tell them the time of the accident, and no doubt, they wouldn't pay out knowing moments before I'd had an accident not on any car, but a big expensive one.

I called Jen, the only person's number I knew by heart. The cop lent me his phone when I told him I had left mine at work. I told her where I was, and she sorted out the tow truck; otherwise, the city would have done it and I would have had to pay an arm and a leg. Something like I would have to do for the car I smashed into; what the fuck was I thinking? I'd been driving for five years and not once had I had an accident. Then again, this one was out of my control. I knew better to speed and brake, my car wasn't an Aston Martin Valkyrie; it was a 1980's Ford I barely managed to have serviced every year, except for this year. When the bonus check came through, I should have used the money to buy a new car, or even better, pay for my insurance but I was fed up with being sensible, and so I took Jen on a little trip to Vegas. She had been my rock from the start when I came to the city jobless and homeless. We met by chance in a coffee shop, when I was going through ads and trying to figure out where I was going to live. I had a job back then; not a great one, but it was enough to get me started in the industry, just not enough for me to live in the city. She told me about a room, her friend was renting. I rented the room, but later on, her friend got married and wanted to sell the place. Either way, I never forgot the kindness she'd shown me back then. She'd been working for Gold for just over two years when I finally joined her in working for him.

Now, I was fucked, not a little, but completely.

"Don't worry, ma'am, he won't hurt you. It's a good thing I got here when I did," the cop said, he spent most of his time talking to my chest and avoiding all eye contact.

I hated whenever men did that. I always felt like taking off my damn shirt and saying, here look some more. You can look all you want, but you can never fucking touch. And the irony of him thinking I should be scared of Ricardo. This cop was eyeing me up like I was some candy, and he had a gun. I wasn't comfortable in his presence and surely didn't feel safe with him.

Ricardo didn't look at me like that, although I could feel his cock growing a little between my legs when he held me so tight. When he took off my door with an ax, it turned me on some. I forgot about how scared and panicked I was about the accident.

Who the fuck had an ax in their car? He did, the tall, dark, hot stranger. I couldn't get my eyes off him, and I didn't know whether to be turned on or scared, which made him even hotter. The way he whisked me over to his car and knew exactly what to do. Even though I had bashed into him and he'd been angry at first, in the midst of it all, he'd been worried about my safety.

"Luckily, he wouldn't do anything to you in public," the cop was saying as I watched my car leave at the side of the curb.

Great, I had to be job hunting on foot. Then again, I could do with losing a few pounds.

"Why? What do you mean?" I asked, wondering what he was going on about.

"Ricardo Ruiz."

"Yeah, the guy I crashed into. The one who saved me from being blown up in my car, yeah him. He's a really bad guy!" I sighed, thinking this cop needed to play a different song; I'd only been here a little while, and Ricardo was the only thing he couldn't stop talking about.

He nodded, "The one and only, and ever since his dad was killed, he's either been in hiding or grieving. Who knows with those animals."

"The big-time mob boss?" I asked as a tremble started low in my gut, making me feel like I was going to throw up, as all the headlines flashed in my mind. Some talked about a turf war, and other news stations praised his death. They didn't show any remorse for it, instead highlighting all the crimes he'd been arrested for. They didn't mention all the times he'd been discharged for being wrongfully accused of the same crime.

"The one and only. Yeah, his dad was carved out like an

animal. I say good to whoever did it. They deserve a medal. They should skin the whole family alive," he smiled proudly.

His dark eyes lit up as he said it, and my eyes glanced at his badge, wondering if it was a fake. He shouldn't be talking to me like this, no, he shouldn't be talking like this at all. He took an oath to serve and obey, not glorify in the slaughter of others.

I wondered if Ricardo would do the same thing to me, the moment he realized my insurance wasn't paid, and I couldn't repair his car.

"Are you ok? You're shaking again?" The cop asked and then he pulled me closer to comfort me. I didn't retaliate because I realized not only had Ricardo's dad been carved up, but he would do the same thing to me. I had believed this day couldn't get any worse, but it just had.

I HAD to take an Uber back home. My skirt was practically ripped all the way to the middle; it was a joke. I couldn't believe I had to give a statement at the station. Jen said it wasn't normal, and it was clear the cop had the hots for me. Which wouldn't bother me so much, if he wasn't creepy. I even thought about inviting him over tonight, so I wouldn't be alone. I was scared of Ricardo. I was fucking petrified; I felt as if all that had happened this morning took place in the space of a year. It was lunchtime and I was hungry, but then I'd lost my appetite the moment I stepped out of the Uber. I couldn't believe who I was seeing outside my apartment block. I slammed the door shut and ran over to her.

"What the heck are you doing here?" I asked Jen as I drew closer, her dark hair with highlights was loose, something I'd told her to do a million times. She always wore it up in a pony-tail as if she was back in high school (so she told me). Her green eyes said it all as she beamed back at me.

"I quit. I couldn't stay after you got fired."

Shit, I had to fill her in. I hadn't been fired, I'd been given two days to determine if I was ready to suck dick or I'd be fired. It was supposedly an option, according to Gold.

"What is it?"

"We need a drink. I haven't exactly been fired. I'll explain it to you once we go upstairs."

"You have wine, right? Lots of it?"

I nodded, "Enough to get us through the day."

She laughed, "and night."

"What about Ben? Is he around or traveling?" She sighed as she talked about her soon to be husband. "Traveling, but he'll be back Friday. So, don't worry I'm all yours and I'll be here all night. After all, I have no job to go back to."

I shook my head as we walked through the lobby, "Yeah, but you have a wedding to plan and pay for. You shouldn't have quit. You shouldn't have done that for me."

I sounded ungrateful. She was sticking up for me, and part of me wondered if I'd deserved such loyalty when I felt like an overgrown child being protected by their mother. She was only a couple of years older than me, but for some reason, she'd felt the need to take care of me from the day we met.

Her parents were comfortable, but compared to mom they were rich, which wasn't hard seeing as she was a single mom with four kids. She was a nurse and we never wanted for anything. When mom died; Jackie, Rebecca, and Alice, my sisters made it clear we didn't have to be in contact anymore. Jackie, only a couple of years older than I, left town straight after the funeral while I was still in college. Rebecca, the eldest, made it clear she didn't want to take on mom's role. She got married, had her own family and turned her back on ours. As for Alice, no one knows; she ran away as soon as she was eighteen. She used to send a postcard to mom, but then they stopped and I remember mom once saying to me, "She was always selfish, only thinking of herself. I knew the cards would stop eventually, I'm not even sure why she bothered sending them in the first place."

No one did.

She would send a card from Vegas, with the big Vegas signs on the front and at the back of the card she would write something like,

I'm here, and you're not.
Alice.

No one knew why she ran away, and after a while, when the postcards stopped coming, no one really cared.

Mom died while I was at college and it was clear all those years of working had taken a toll on her. I missed her every single day and promised I would work hard to make her proud of me, which was more than I could say about my sisters. I hadn't seen two of them since the funeral, which was four years ago. It was as if once mom died, we didn't feel the need to stay in touch. It was sad, but a harsh reality was we were happy when we didn't have to be in each other's company. In a way, Jen reminds me of the sister I never had, the type of relationship I'd wished I'd had with at least one of my sisters.

She pressed the elevator button, and I clutched my purse.

She waved her hand as she said, "You don't have to worry about me paying for the wedding, Dad will take care of it. After all, he's the father of the bride."

I dipped my head, "Didn't think they still did it that way."

She smiled, "They do. Urgh, is your roommate coming back tonight?"

I shook my head, "Oh, I forgot to tell you." The doors opened, and we stepped inside, and I pressed the button to go up to the top floor.

"She went to 321 and now she has herself a boyfriend. You

went there and found your soul mate, two years ago. I went there, too, but all I've ever done is met jerks. Anyway, apparently, he lives downtown in an apartment much nicer than hers, so she's there nearly all the time."

She shivered, "What's up with this dude? Rich. Probably hot, too, and he's dating her. She makes Blair Waldorf from *Gossip Girl* seem nice."

I shrugged, "I've only met him once and to tell you the truth, he was a male version of her."

I didn't go into too much detail, but it was no secret my roommate, Debbie, had an air about her as if she was better than everyone else, including me. She was rich, and had no job, but her dad cut down her allowance, forcing her to rent out a room, to get some extra income. Jen never really came over here for this reason, but it was tough getting someone to rent out a room in the city, most wanted to rent out their whole apartment, something I couldn't afford to pay.

"Explains it. I couldn't imagine her going out with a nice guy, she would eat him alive!"

"Exactly," I said, thinking Jen had summed them both up in the short sentence.

The elevator doors opened and as we got out, I started to search for my keys in my bag, which was too big, and held nearly all my world belongings in it, such as my passport, make-up, wipes and everything else.

"I'm glad you're okay. I was a little worried. I know how hard you worked to keep it going for just one more year," she said.

I shook my head as I finally found my keys and opened the door.

"I need to fill you in on the rest of the day, I'll get the wine, some chips and then we'll talk."

I shut the door behind me as I held my breath and dumped my bag on the floor. I couldn't be bothered to put it in my room. Debbie hated it when I did that, but she wasn't here, and I had so much to tell Jen, especially seeing as I didn't know if today would be my last day on the earth after the accident I'd just had.

∽

"ALL THIS HAPPENED before eleven this morning?"

I dipped my head. After sipping my second glass, no more was my ripped skirt bothering me. I'd completely ripped it down the middle. It was just covering my thighs down the sides. I didn't care, it was the least of my worries.

"Why didn't you tell me about your insurance? I could have covered it. Wait. No, no, no...we didn't have to go to Vegas. You could have paid for the insurance instead."

I nodded, "I know, but I rely on you too much. Now, I wish I hadn't called to tell you about the car or even Gold's offer."

She started to go through her purse, as she tried to get up and missed her balance and ended up tumbling on the floor. We both laughed until she handed it to me. A brand new XR iPhone, still in its box, she handed it to me, as she slumped on the brown leather sofa.

"This is too much; I'll get a phone."

"They took my phone, too, so I bought it on the way not only for you, but for me too. Besides you kept a back-up of everything in the iCloud, so it makes sense to have a personal iPhone. This way you can still keep all your contacts, photos and stuff."

"Holy crap, I forgot about the photos. Yeah, it makes sense. Seriously, I'll never repay you with all the money you spend on me. Anyway, it doesn't matter I may not need a phone or a job if Ruiz carves me up alive! Like they did with his dad."

I handed her the once empty glass, which I refilled while talking. We were both sitting on the floor of the two-bedroom apartment.

I could move further out of town, and get something cheaper, which would be another option, I remembered one time looking at the classified section and seeing studio apartments going for the same price I was paying for my room. Or maybe they were a little more. I couldn't remember. I wasn't in the right frame of mind to be thinking of such things; I was too busy drinking rather than eating chips, and she was doing the same thing.

She laughed, "What, you think you're so important he would send one of his men to take care of you? Because you crashed your car at the back of his, you lost your job, and you lied about your insurance. I'm sure they have bigger fish to fry."

"Thanks for making me feel so important."

She laughed, "I can't believe you slapped Carrie. Damn, if I wish I could have been on a fly on the precious white walls."

"What she said was cruel and uncalled for. Anyway, I'm too damn nervous about Ruiz. Shit, why didn't I put two and two together and realize it was him."

"Please. You're not important. Most likely he won't even bother with the insurance, you'll have nothing to worry about. Besides didn't you say he drives an Aston Martin Valkyrie?"

"Yeah, I've never been close to one before and you know the worst part is I think his car barely had a scratch on it. Whereas mine was completely a write-off."

She laughed, "You had masking tape at the front to keep it together, and you vowed the masking tape was good enough to hold the car together. It was a write-off before the accident!"

I flopped on to the cream rug floor, it was so soft and gentle, "I know. Crazy right? It was up in smoke, and his just had a scratch on it. If even that."

I agreed as I sat up, "Anyway, you're right he wouldn't bother with the insurance for a scratch. And he saw my car was beaten up."

She waved her finger up in the air, "You could get him for

using his ax against your car. You could countersue him for damages."

"I'm scared he's going to kill me. He has an ax in his car, and you want me to countersue? You really want me to die!"

We both laughed, so hard I nearly knocked over the small glass table in the middle of the two sofas. Seeing the glass table reminded me of Gold and Carrie.

"As for Gold, he can forget it. I'm not going anywhere near him."

She pulled closer to me, as she tried to carefully move the table out of the way. Red wine, and a cream Persian rug did not mix. For sure Debbie would kick me out of the apartment, rent paid or not. I never came in here, only when she wasn't around, otherwise, she would be on me for leaving a mess. So, I mainly stuck to using the bathroom, hardly cooked in the kitchen, and spent most of my time in my room.

"Is it true about his weight-loss? Does he look completely different?"

I rose an eyebrow, "He does, but when you know a person, what they're like, it doesn't matter how much weight they lose, they still look ugly."

She sighed, "Poor Linda, his wife, putting up with him."

I choked. "It's clear the money keeps her going, I mean, she must know what he's like."

"True. Do you have any real food to eat?" As she struggled to get up, she knew better than to ask me. I always had snacks, nibbles, and wine on hand, a little too much on hand lately. Loneliness had taken over my body and mind, which was part of the reason I screwed up the presentations. I was introduced to my roommate's boyfriend, whom she'd met at the same club Jen and I went to, when we vowed to get a man in the city. The problem was Jen did, while every man I met wanted one thing. There was no, 'hey beautiful, you wanna dance?' which was what Ben said to Jen. It was, 'you wanna get out of here?' or one time, 'the men's free, if you want to go with me.' Yep, they wanted one thing and they didn't hide it, either, this was the sad part about it, and it made my self-esteem plummet.

"I want to make them payyyyy," I slurred, as I finally figured out how to get off the floor and started heading to the open-plan white kitchen, which was a bitch to clean.

She sat on the bench as she faced me, ready to be dazzled with something to eat.

"Puff, chocolate, muffins, croissant, or nuts?"

She shrugged, "A little of each, then we can get something decent to eat from the take-out later, or we could go out?"

I backed up and pointed to my ripped skirt, "In this?"

She shook her head, "No, you'd have to change."

I sighed, "Nah, I can't be bothered, this could be my last meal. I want to be in the comfort of my own home."

"Veronica, you're too dramatic."

I laughed, but I had a feeling I wasn't being dramatic, I didn't think Ricardo would sweep it under the carpet, as much as I hoped he would.

10

R icardo

ANOTHER DEAD END!

Fuck, this day was supposed to be a good one, giving up some positive leads. If I didn't find my dad's killer and take revenge, I was a dead man.

Fuck, I could hear them already. He couldn't even find his dad's killer. He's done. We should take him out.

Either way, I would be taken out.

Damned if I did; damned if I didn't find the killer.

I disturbed Jose as I wiped the blood off my hand and heard the whimpers from Pete's throat. He was one of the lookouts on the North side. He worked for whoever was paying the better price. He was one of those types who had no real loyalty and was only interested in green. No one would miss him, so I knew I could get information out of him, and if I didn't, then I could dump him, and his spot would be replaced in a heartbeat by the Lopez family. They preferred hiring their own, so realistically I was doing them a favor. Pete wasn't as sharp as he used to be. The man should have been out of the business a long time ago. He was hitting sixty, but still hit the strip clubs and brothels like a fucking teenager.

"Hospital or morgue?" Jose asked as he rubbed his bald head, and his eyes darted to mine, probably wondering if Pete would make the journey out of here. I had given him a good thrashing. I'd had a shit day, needed to take my frustration out on someone, and someone just happened to be Pete.

I shrugged. "Whatever?"

He patted me on the back and said, "Boss, don't lose hope, I think Mario will come through for us."

I sighed, thinking about it. The more dead ends I was coming to, the more I was convinced a woman had killed Pa. There was nothing worse than a woman scorned, and Pa's attitude with women was a unique one. One I wasn't proud of.

"Good news about the cop. We taught him a lesson y the girl, the one who crashed into the back of your car..." He paused for a minute as he checked to see if Pete was still breathing.

"Right. Taking this one to the hospital, and as for the girl, she's got no insurance."

I laughed. "Why would she have insurance for the beat-up Ford? Even the damn side mirrors were held up with tape."

Out of breath as he held Pete's lifeless body, he asked, "So, why did you want me to check up on her?"

I could have told him, confided in him, but there was a time and place for everything. He needed to get Pete to the hospital, so I got him to check-up on Veronica as I got to the restaurant and decided to get everything I could out of Pete. I kept Jose occupied while I did. He was a whiz on the computer and had access to most police systems and even the military's, too. He could have gone to college to study to be some computer whiz, but he wanted to help out the family, unlike Juan. Jose loved being a part of this life. Sometimes, I called him in just to give Juan a hand, like I'd done today.

"Never mind," I said quietly.

"Hey, Juan, help lift him. Don't drag him or we'll have to go to the morgue after getting to the hospital. I'm only making one trip today."

Juan shrugged, the same as he did every time you tried to talk to him. He was the same height and had the same dark eyes as Jose, but you would think Jose was at least ten years older. He drank too much, smoked a little more, and didn't eat well at all. He was what we would call in Mexico, *friganismo*. A person who eats like trash. Also, Jose loved to spend a little too much time in front of the computer, hacking and messing up systems just for the fun of it. He got a buzz out of it. Most people didn't even realize he and Juan were twins because Juan looked younger and healthier. He tried to get his brother to change his ways, but sometimes there's no helping some people.

"I'm gone. You guys do what you have to do," I said and Juan fling the body at the back of the truck as if it was a piece of meat. I shook my head after Jose made it clear they were taking him to the hospital. Jose checked him again and sighed, "Nice going Juan. Now we have to take him to the morgue."

Juan shrugged as I expected him to do. As fascinating as it was watching the two of them, I had more important business to take care of. I had been hoping Veronica Smith wouldn't have insurance, and I had been right. She could be what I need to take the edge off at the moment. I had craved her from the moment I saw her, and unfortunately Pete, who was now at the back of the trunk, was reaping the proceeds of my frustration. She could be what I needed to put everything in place for a while.

A muse.

A toy.

A secret weapon.

I couldn't decide on which one, but I would do as much, once I got myself home and had a nice long shower and a couple of shots to knock me out for the night. xxx

11

eronica

I HAD a hangover and was still in my ripped skirt, not the most attractive sight when the door buzzed. It was weird because usually, I would have to buzz them up to the apartment, unless Debbie forgot her key. She did sometimes, but if that's what had happened, who'd let her into the building? Maybe someone had been coming out and she had been coming in. Either way, I stepped over Jen and headed to the door. My hair was a mess, I didn't smell great, and I looked even worse.

I should have used the damn peephole; after all, but with my head all screwed up, the only thing I could think about was opening the door, nothing more.

I swung the door open, and before me was Ricardo. The same one I smashed into, here on the other side of the door.

"Hello," I whispered, trying to cover myself up. His emerald eyes flashed over my body and he was in a black suit, just like he had been yesterday. All dark and mysterious, but this time he had a bit of stubble, something I hadn't noticed about him earlier.

He didn't wait for me to invite him in, moving past me and inviting himself in.

"I see you have company." His gaze darted to the floor, where Jen was attempting to crawl onto the sofa.

I dipped my head, feeling as if I was at his place and I had to tidy up quickly. I dashed to move the bottle from the floor, then the other which was on the glass table, and then put them in the closest, as if I was being caught drinking and I was underage. It was a stupid move, the boxes from the Chinese takeout were on the sofa, Debbie would kill me. I quickly stood by the closet, eying everything else that needed tidying up.

"I'll make it quick," he blurted.

I tried to avoid looking at his green eyes, but they were like a magnet. I couldn't get away from them, or from his olive skin and black suit, everything was black and then I got wondering, if his boxers were black too, or if he had any on.

"You have no insurance. You don't own this place, you merely rent it; just one room and you're jobless. How will you pay for the damage to my car?"

Fuck! He did want me to pay, I had been hoping he would let it go. I was tempted to tell him he didn't need the money from me; he could go get it from someone else, kill them for it. But then I didn't want to give him any ideas, so I kept my mouth shut.

"You have two choices. Figure out how to pay, or give me payment in another form."

There was nothing to figure out. I didn't need to go online to figure out the damage to his car, would cost more than the two hundred and fifty dollars I had in my account.

"Technically, you only have one choice. For sure, you don't possess twenty-five thousand to repair the scratch on my Aston

Martin. Neither can you afford to have your car shipped to the scrapyard because the garage it was sent to will not repair it. It's damaged beyond repair. So, I had it shipped to the dump. I did you a favor."

Did he want me to curtsy or get on my hands and knees and praise his kindness? He knew everything about me. I bet he knew what color underwear I was wearing now. Shit, he could see it. My skirt had ripped through, and he knew what I was doing as I looked down and tried to dignify myself, but I couldn't because he drew so close, I could smell his woodsy cologne and the fresh mint scent was slowly putting me into a trance.

He didn't give me a chance to do anything, as he growled, "You have no choice. You'll have to come and stay with me for thirty days. My driver will come and pick you in an hour."

Then he backed away from me, I tried to regain my thoughts, told them to get out of the gutter, as much as my panties were wet, maybe because I was scared or because he was turning me on. Either way, Jen moaned as if she was in the comfort of her bed, as she laid on the sofa. She wasn't a part of this conversation, she was in her own little world, one far away from here.

"What? I don't understand." I was brought to earth as I repeated the words which came out of his mouth in my head.

No more was I aroused, but angry, every man just seemed to think I was ready to do sexual favors. This was different than it had been with Gold. This one was probably a survival tactic. The meaning of life or death.

"Because for the next thirty days," he came closer to me again and I tried to move away, but then I was against the kitchen counter. "You'll be the price for repairing my car. I'll own you. Possess you. Be ready in an hour. Don't keep my driver waiting."

Then he moved away from me and shut the door behind

him. I stood in confusion for a full minute, head reeling. I didn't know what it was about this man. I should have been scared after what he said to me, but I wasn't because my panties were dripping wet.

"I THINK I sobered up in all of five minutes. Was that him?"

I nodded as Jen held on to me, as she tried to straighten up. I think my encounter with him sobered her up as fast as it had done with me.

"He's hot. So hot. Gee, if you won't go for thirty days, I'll go for thirty months in your place," Jen said as she scrolled through the few pictures of him on her phone.

I shook my head. "You're not going anywhere. You're soon to be a married woman." I led her to the bar stool in the kitchen and she happily sat down as I looked at the digital clock in the kitchen, thinking I had exactly forty-five minutes to get ready before his driver got here.

"He's hot. Like super-hot. Imagine, for thirty days he'll be taking you out shopping, treating you like a princess. How many times have we watched *365 Days*?"

I laughed. "Enough to know it'll more likely end up like Stephen King's *Misery* and I'll be locked in a room, fed by him, and treated like a prisoner."

Damn, the idea of it was still making me wet. What the heck was wrong with me?

"You need to have a long shower and tell roommate dearest you're moving out. Get your shit together, or even better burn it and then we're out of here."

She started to get off the stool.

"Where are you going?"

She laughed. "Home to pack. You need someone to watch your back."

I repeated, "Not you, you're getting married!"

She insisted, "Not in thirty days I'm not."

I knew she was kidding, but the idea of her coming with me, as if to say, *hey, Ricardo you have two for the price of one* was absurd. I didn't think that was what he meant when he said to be ready in an hour. Shit, forty-four minutes.

"Time is ticking and you're playing games. He's not the type to play games with."

I dipped my head, thinking she was right, I had to get ready; realistically, I had no choice but to go. As he said, I had one of two options; then he said, oh, wait, you only have one!

"I'll go through your closet while you're showering and sort out what you need, then the rest of your stuff I'll have sent to mine. Ok?"

I shook my head, "Why? You think he's going to kill me?"

She said, "Don't be silly, if he was going to kill you, he would have done it by now. No, Ricardo wants you for other reasons; he has the hots for you. I'm sure of, otherwise, he wouldn't be sending his driver, or want you at his convenience for thirty days. He wouldn't be making the offer if he didn't; so it's all good."

I still wasn't convinced as we moved from the kitchen to my room.

"Think of *Beauty and the Beast*. He kept Bella locked up and look at the result."

I laughed. "My life's not a fairy tale, and I need to take out these damn contacts."

She sighed as she held on to my face, "No one's life is a fairytale, but you need to be realistic. He wants you in his house for thirty days, and to do what? Clean dishes?

During the time, you won't be able to pay rent or anything, and you need time to look for a job. So, in the meantime, I'll keep your stuff at my place and you can give Debbie notice.

Better still, I'll do it for you. You don't have much time. It'll all work out."

Then she hugged me and gave me a light kiss on the cheek. I turned and walked towards the bathroom, ready to take a much-needed shower. Ricardo didn't want to kill me now, so it was all good. All I needed to do was keep him happy for thirty days, so he wouldn't kill me by the end of it. Then again, if I kept him too happy, he may decide he wanted me for a lot longer than thirty days.

Jen was my voice of reason, I just had to get ready to leave. Thinking about my predicament wasn't really an option. Options were lost the moment I crashed into the back of the Mexican mob boss's car.

12

eronica

JEN HAD a shower and changed into my sweats. Everything seemed to be going according to plan until the buzzer rang, and I knew it was my time to leave.

"Don't look so nervous, and you'll be fine."

I dipped my head like a child being sent to school for the first time. Worried, unsure about the whole day, and even more scared about being alone. I always worked so hard; I never surrounded myself with friends. Even as a kid. Mom always complained about me being alone all the time, she would say *it's not healthy, you need to make friends sometimes.* I didn't take after either mom or my sisters; they all had an influx of friends. I enjoyed my alone time a lot more than I enjoyed being around people; until I became friends with Jen. I didn't know what I would do without her.

I took a deep breath as we both stood behind the door and I

opened it. I was shocked by his driver. I expected some old guy, ex-army or some goon, tall and big looking and especially scary to be standing on the other side. Instead, I was greeted by someone who didn't even look old enough to drive and he was wearing a T-shirt and jeans. He had enough tattoos to make Justin Bieber appear to be tattoo-less, and the more I thought about it, if his hair was a little longer and lighter, he could easily have been Bieber's twin.

"Hey, you're Veronica, right?" he asked, chewing gum.

I dipped my head and even Jen was speechless.

"Cool, 'cuz said you had dark hair, but he didn't give me much to go on. Anyway, you reds?"

I assumed he meant ready, so once again I nodded and turned to kiss and face Jen.

She whispered, "See, it's not all bad. He sent a kid to pick you up."

Yeah, I may have dramatized the situation in my head, I had ideas about some army guy coming to pick me up and threatening me with a gun to my head or even telling me to get in the car by knocking us out. He would drag my lifeless body to the car, and I'd wake up to find out I'd been chained to the bed. Yeah, Jen was right; we'd been watching too much *CSI*, *NCSI*, the *Sopranos* and all the movies which painted a different picture than the one I was facing right now.

"If I were you, I wouldn't even bother taking this much. I'm sure Ric will be buying you new stuff."

I smiled, as Justin's twin taking my suitcase out. He was strong; he wasn't even using the rollers and he was holding it as if it was a feather.

"See, told you. Enjoy and once you've finished living in the land of luxury, then I'll be waiting for you."

It was nice to know someone would wait for me. I'd packed the phone she bought me and promised to text her every night. I started to get teary, like I did when I left home, but for the same reason. I wasn't upset about leaving my sisters, the town or the house, which I used to call home. No, it was all about mom. I hated not being there when she'd finished her night shift and was so tired, she would sit in the kitchen, while I made her breakfast, then I'd help her to bed and kiss her good night before going to school. My first worry when I left home was she wouldn't get any more kisses before going to bed. I worried if she'd even have a meal before hitting the sack. I found out at the funeral I was right to worry; she didn't get any of those things once I left.

"Stop it, or you'll get me started. You'll be back." Jen smiled at me reassuringly.

"I know, but I'm so used to seeing your face every day."

She laughed, "If it makes you feel better, video call me at night."

I nodded, "I will."

Then I let go of her and decided she was right. I had no job to come back to, so it made no sense to stay in this apartment. I hated the idea of being her roommate when she was going to be married soon, but in six months, she'd be married and move into her new house. They were in the process of buying, so I had nothing to feel guilty about. I hated the idea of being forced to do something when I was always in control.

"The elevator doors are waiting for you to jump in."

I ran to the doors, thinking the longer I dragged leaving, the more I would cry and regret agreeing to it all. Even if I didn't have a choice in the matter. I wore my black shift dress, but I kept my stomach in, otherwise, it would be clear it didn't fit, and I'd squeezed into it. It hugged my breasts in a bit, and anyone who said black made you look a slimmer wasn't lying. This dress made me feel a lot lighter, as it hugged me in all the right places.

"I thought you had changed your mind," the driver laughed

as he held on to the button. As soon as I entered the elevator, I replied, "I thought I had no choice but to go."

All of a sudden, he didn't look cute anymore as his once bright eyes, all of a sudden turned dark as he agreed, "True, if Ric tells you to come, then you come. If you want to stay alive."

A cold shiver ran down my spine as I deliberated about the idea I'd had before he came. A gun being held to my head and being dragged to the car. The idea this was all some romantic gesture made me feel stupid. Sometimes, I needed to grow up and see life for what it was. It wasn't a big fairytale. This was my reality, as Jen said. I had to survive the next thirty days and get out. My escape plan would be to leave Chicago, the city I'd grown to love. I couldn't stay here after my time was up; I could only hope I survived this ordeal and had a choice in my decisions once again after it was all over.

"My name's Diego, by the way. But you can call me, D. Most folks do."

I dipped my head, but I was speechless. In the space of a few minutes, he'd told me indirectly, if I didn't go with him, Ricardo would kill me, and had then moved to exchanging names.

"I'll be taking you to the main house, which is a ride out of the city. So, if you want to make a pit stop or get something to eat, shout."

I nodded as he took my case, and I clutched my purse. I didn't know why I was doing it, maybe nerves. It wasn't as if D would steal my purse.

"I'm not sure if Ric's coming to the house tonight, maybe not. But I can't wait around. I've got things to do."

He said casually as we walked through the lobby. He was chatty, which should have put my mind at ease, but for some reason it did the complete opposite. My mind was racing in all types of directions as I was thinking about my escape plans.

"Okay."

He stopped as we reached the doors, as if he was studying me, and it made me feel anxious.

"I'll give you a few pointers. Ric is not like me at all. But what he doesn't like is the feeling everyone's scared of him. I'm as laidback as anyone else in our circle and it's why he sent me. If he wanted to intimidate you, then he would have sent Juan. If he wanted to take you out, Jose. Me, I'm the guy if he sends to make you feel at home. It's not often he wants that, but if he does, then the person's kind of special to him. You get me?"

I dipped my head as his eyes moved to my purse I was clutching as if my life depended on it. My knees were shaking and I was wondering if he could hear my teeth chatter, too. Most people in this building worked, so I didn't have the embarrassment of someone passing and seeing me nearly pee my pants. No, Diego would be the only one to have the pleasure and as I dipped my head and tried to remember to breathe, I followed him out of the building and into the limo parked outside.

"Wow, we're going there in style."

He smiled, "That's better, a little bit of excitement. Seriously, I know some guys and even women have worked for Ric for like ten years, they've never been to the main house, so you've definitely made an impression, a good one. There's nothing to worry about."

He was right, I hadn't been threatened, if anything I would have to agree with Jen, I had been given the star treatment. I didn't have a job and until I did, it made sense to leave the apartment. When I called Debbie to tell her I was moving out, I had asked her for a refund on the remainder of this month. She'd hung up saying *good*, which meant, she planned to rent the place out. She wasn't going to be living there long, which is why she was never there. It made sense; I'd seen Jen do the same thing with Ben; they start dating and slowly, but surely one of the two apartments became practically empty. Diego opened the door and I climbed in, and as I sat down I ran my fingers over the white leather seats.

"Oh my," I purred as the back opened and Diego stuffed my case at the back. I felt like a little girl being left alone in a toy store, able to play with as many things as I could get my hands on. I opened the bar and saw the range of drinks from water and soda to alcohol. There were even a few snacks, chips, and nuts. It was like being in first-class on a plane. Not that I'd ever had the luxury, but if I had, I was pretty sure it would feel like this.

"Help yourself to anything in the bar. As I said, if you want to stop and do some lady stuff, or go somewhere on the way, then your wish is my command," Diego said as he rolled down the window dividing us both.

I smiled and said, "Let's get this show on the road."

The limo pulled out, and I poured myself a glass of chardonnay. It was amazing seeing the city from a different point of view. The way all rich people did, when they sat at the back of the limo with darkened windows. They saw everything and people like me, normal people, didn't get to see them. The shoe would be on the other foot, and I intended to sit back and enjoy the ride.

13

R icardo

"JEFE, how long we going to Italy for?" Juan's question disturbed my thoughts as I looked out of the window.

"One night."

It was all it would take, one night to find the woman I needed to help me finish my quest.

Juan buckled up and put his head back. "Okay." Then he closed his eyes and drifted off to sleep. He deserved it. It was going to be a long ride, and I should be catching some z's too, but I was too wound up. In an ideal world, I would have had Veronica sent to the house, had her prepped and the next day, been with her, but Pa's death was a mystery I had to get some outside help with.

I couldn't get it in Chicago, certainly not in Mexico because as much as I loved my people, they had big mouths. Someone,

66

somewhere would blab. I had never felt like this before, unsure, unclear of the future and it was making me fucking nervous. I hadn't thought I could feel this way about anything until now.

"Would you like a drink, Señor Ruiz, from the bar?"

I shook my head as the dark-haired air stewardess tried to offer me a drink, but as I turned and my eyes danced on her chest, I could tell she was offering me a lot more than something to drink. Half of the buttons on her uniform were undone, and her breasts were on display.

"No."

She looked disappointed, not only by what I said, but the fact I turned my head and continued to stare out of the window. I couldn't look at her, as memories about the last time I was on dad's private jet assailed me. He had sat right where Juan was sitting right now, but Pa wasn't snoring like a pig as he did three months ago, yet it felt like only yesterday.

"The youth are completely lost," Pa smiled at me, at the time I thought he was referring to me, but as he continued to speak, I knew exactly who and what he meant.

"Look at Diego. His mom was a nurse and he's been in this business long enough to know we're not in the habit of fixing things, but taking what we need and moving on."

I sighed. "Pa, he's not that bad."

He shook his head. "He's got everything mixed up and upside down. His focus is all over the place, and I worry...."

It was as if he was struggling for words, and curiosity got the better of me as I asked the question.

"Qué?"

He stared at me for a brief second as if I'd woken him up from a deep sleep.

"When he breaks, it'll be nasty."

I still didn't get it so I repeated, my question, "Que?"

"He'll be more ruthless and deadly than both of us

combined, mark my words. This is why youth like him have to be trained, to be tamed. They have to be shown the right way, so they know they can't make up their own rules."

"Pa, don't worry. I'll train him."

I remembered thinking at the time about the friendly, happy-go-lucky side of Diego and the loyalty part, too. I couldn't see him turning into something dark, but I wasn't a fortune teller, and I must admit dad was better at judging personalities than I was, so I made it my duty to keep an eye on him, seeing as how it was his mother who had been wrongfully killed when a turf war started. When the driver told her to get out of the car and run, she was taken out because she couldn't do it. She couldn't leave someone who was a patient; she was a nurse. She'd died as the Pastors gunned her down. They said that it was her fault innocents always got caught in the crossfire. Pa said that even if she had run, it wouldn't have made a difference. Either way, he made the family pay for their mistaken identity error.

"You're a good leader, Hijo!"

He smacked my knee in a friendly gesture as if to make me feel like I had a chance, but realistically I knew from this talk, it was out of my hand. Pa didn't want to tell me the truth, but I was on a mission to prove him wrong.

As I deliberated about his statement about me being a good leader, a tear welled up in my eye. I had to get my head out of the clouds while thinking about the past, and only move forward. If all went well, not only would the woman in Italy be helping me, but Veronica would be too, so once and for all I could put my Pa to rest and bury him. Until that, day, I would keep him on ice because I had a job to do. Nothing could be put to rest until it was done.

~

I SHUT my eyes for what felt like a few seconds, but must have been a lot longer because once again we were on land. I loved Sicily. I'd been here a few times, Pa had some good contacts here, and we came here whenever we wanted discretion, and we were never disappointed about the speed and the quality of the work done.

Besides, I needed to get out of the city for a few days. I felt as if I'd swam out too far and I was drowning in the ocean. I hadn't slept or eaten since I'd seen his body; it still haunted me, the idea of him suffering so much.

"Buongiorno," the pilot said as he stood by my side, and I realized not only were we on land, but we'd come to a complete stop.

"I hope the flight was to your satisfaction."

I dipped my head. "It was."

"Jefe? We're here," Juan said, as if he'd been woken from a nightmare.

"Yeah, we're here."

I took in a deep breath, unbuckled my seatbelt, and attempted to get out of my seat. I collapsed back into it, struggling to get up. I was exhausted, and the idea of having a conversation, then jumping back on the plane was too much.

"Juan, book us a hotel for the night. I need to lie down."

He smiled and said, "About time. You need to rest. Your eyes are red, you're slow in talking, slower than me. You need to rest, Jefe. Just take one night off."

As we settled into a taxi bound for the hotel, I opened the file on Veronica. Even after nearly two years of living in the city, Veronica didn't have many friends, only her best friend Jen. The file on her was clear, she worked and had no social life outside of work. She was from a small town in Iowa, but even then her mom became pregnant at a young age and married the boy whose parents owned the local diner. Her mom had decided to study nursing, but for some reason she'd done all the work, whereas her husband sat back and did nothing. Then, his parents died, leaving him the money from the diner, he ran off and left her with not one kid, but three.

Her dad resided in California. He had a new wife, and kid. A new family. Also, he had a brother, and they weren't in touch. As for her mom's family, they seemed to be a complete mystery. They left town when she married Veronica's dad, and disappeared, which most likely meant they were killed. Maybe an accident, maybe they got caught up in something they couldn't handle. No one disappears like that, especially people from Iowa who were not involved in any illegal activity.

There were no photos of Veronica going back home on her social media, which was strange in this day and age. Especially seeing as she had three sisters. One of whom seemed to love working in strip clubs in Vegas, and had a nasty drug addict. Another was a reporter in NY. The other was happily married with twins. None of them had anything on their social media about Veronica, or even the other sister. It's as if they were all only children. The crazy part is Alice, the one who loved working in strip clubs, was on her social media profile day and night. It's as if she wanted someone to find out where she was and what she was doing, twenty-four/seven.

You could tell so much about someone by looking up their Facebook or Instagram page. The latest seemed to be TikTok, but Veronica didn't have an account. Veronica's holidays consisted of only one trip to Vegas. Her job with Gold was a result of a chance meeting, and she even posted of it completely changing her life.

Everything would change, including Veronica. She would be taken care of, and I would tell Diego to see to it. Most importantly the woman I was meeting would have to wait. I didn't feel well; it was as if my stomach was in knots and I knew it was a mix of drinking and not eating and having all the weight of the world on my shoulders. I could feel the heat as the jet doors opened, and it made me feel even more tired. I could have had a coffee or something to keep me awake, but I wanted to sleep. I needed to rest, so I could do things with a clear mind, and not a frustrated one.

14

V eronica

I WAS ALONE in the room, with no one to talk to, so I quickly shuffled through my purse. Dropping it, I took out my phone and called Jen. I didn't check the time to make sure it was okay to call her. I just had to see her friendly face, so I decided not only to call her, but to FaceTime her instead.

"Hey, you okay?" she asked, as she picked up the call.

"Yeah, the room I've been given is nearly the size of my apartment. No, my old apartment," I said as I moved the phone around, so she could see the double-sized closest at the back of the room, the Turkish rug, the double doors leading to the balcony so I could sit outside when the weather was nicer and face the ground, and an amazing bathroom. It had a walk-in shower, an antique tub at the corner, and a splash of both a modern and antique feel to it. It was nice.

"You seen him yet?"

"No. Diego said...you know the driver who picked me up," I laid on the bed, thinking I would fill her in, about my ride and the trail of events until this moment.

"Okay, that's his name."

"Yeah, he said most likely I wouldn't see him till Friday at this rate or sometime over the weekend, so it's all a guessing game at the moment," I said, repeating what Diego said as he introduced me to Lourdes, the housekeeper who then showed me my room. It was clear, I wasn't going to see Diego again, well not for now, he left the house repeating I would be okay and Lourdes would take care of me.

"Well, it's not such a bad thing, you can relax a bit, and..."

"Do what?" I sighed, noticing she was all dressed up and ready to go out. It was a Wednesday night, her date night with Ben. I could tell by the way she was waving her hand, she had to go, but didn't want to leave me, not when I was looking so down.

I sat up and put a smile on my face. "You should get going. Date night, right?"

She nodded. "Yeah, but you look so sad, even underneath the fake smile."

She knew me too well, part of me loved her for it, but it made me feel guilty, knowing I was stopping her from enjoying herself.

"So, where are you going tonight?"

She smiled. "It's a surprise; not sure yet."

I loved that about Ben, he knew how to keep the romance going. I hoped once they were married he would keep giving her the element of surprise. Well, it worked both ways. She did the same for him in the bedroom department with her constant visits to the sex shop. I went with her a few times because it always amused me how open they were about sex. Something that had been a closed topic in my family. We never openly talked about sex, and I believed it was normal. Mom never asked if I was a virgin, and I never asked her what to do if I met a guy.

"Well, I know you'll surprise him back," I winked at her, reminding her about the sexy lingerie she bought last weekend.

She laughed, and I knew we could spend all night on the call, but she had a date. I had to let her go.

"Have a good time, and I have a book I need to catch up on. I'll be fine. I'm in a mansion, with a housekeeper. What more could a girl ask for?"

She agreed, and we hung up. I was right, I hadn't eaten and I was feeling a little hungry, so I would go on a hunt to try and find Lourdes and snoop a bit. Maybe there were other people in this house and I didn't know where they were, and they didn't know I was here, either.

Diego did say I should feel as if I was Ricardo's guest and not his prisoner, and I intended to do just that as I jumped off the bed and put on my shoes to go and explore the house.

15

R icardo

I WOKE up and I felt as if I'd been asleep for only a couple of hours. I checked the time to realize it was nearly lunchtime. I had been exhausted, and the silk sheets and king-size bed had knocked me out. As well as the shot of sherry I had before hitting the sack. I felt alive, more alive than I'd felt in weeks. I didn't feel as if the world was on my shoulders as I stretched and got out of bed.

Shit, I wish I could spend one more night here, just to feel like myself one more time. Maybe it was the stress of being at home that had, stopped me from sleeping, and not the grief.

I headed to the shower in my birthday suit. I always slept in the nude, but didn't even bother drawing the blinds as I headed there. I clicked on the light as I went. My memory was good, but not good enough to remember what direction I was headed in. One thing I hated was showering with the light on. There was something about bathing in the dark which felt natural to me. I turned on the tap and instantly, the steam formed. Damn, it was quick.

I stepped in and the water was too hot, so I adjusted the temperature and felt even better as I hit the perfect temperature, the light in the room just enough for me to figure out where the sponge Juan must have put in here ready for me to start my day. Not only was he loyal, but he knew my creature habits. I had a habit of getting up and going in the shower and having everything ready for me., I didn't want to have to worry about finding the soap and such, and it was that little attention to detail he always took care of which made me always travel with him.

Juan didn't have anyone but his brother. Both his parents were dead, and he'd never found love. I did wonder if he played for the other team, so I asked him about his love life and he said he'd loved once, and it was enough for any man to have one love of his life. I didn't ask what happened to her, and he never told me. Some things didn't need to be said, and broken hearts was a topic most men avoided talking about like the plague.

As soon as I was done in the bathroom, it was time for breakfast, and as expected, my expresso and sliced toast were waiting for me. I didn't eat much in the morning and at times I would skip the toast and opt for only fruit. But I hadn't eaten last night and had hardly anything the day before, so both the toast and the fruit basket in front of me were welcome.

Now, it was time to draw the blinds and see the view I was told last night by reception rented this room for $600 per night. So, it better be fucking good. As the blinds lifted, I had to agree it was worth every penny. There was a beautiful blue clear sky with the few clouds hanging as if they were magically painted in the sky. The deep blue sea, and the apartment and office buildings looked as if they were stacked next to each other and not on top of each other like in Chicago. The hunger I once felt, soon went away as I opened the window and took in the fresh air. I didn't smell pollution, only the Mediterranean Sea breeze. Then I looked to my right to see the cliff and debated staying one more night. Maybe I would go for a hike to the top and see the island from a different angle, a beauty I couldn't resist. All I had seen and felt recently was ugliness; this could be my proof that life wasn't full of darkness.

I lifted my coffee, unable to pull myself away from the view, and somewhere in the midst of my thoughts, Veronica crossed my mind. I had her at home waiting for me, and I didn't want to return there. I needed to stay here. It was as if the thought was repeating in my mind, but men like me didn't take vacations; no, I had a job to do. I couldn't fucking take a break when there was a reason why I was here, and I needed Veronica. Not only to satisfy my needs, but to get the job done.

I stopped daydreaming, finished my expresso, took a couple of bites of a banana and decided to get ready to meet her. The one who would help me put an end to it all and catch Pa's killer.

I HATED TARDINESS, it was one thing Pa would say didn't make me a Mexican. If I had to wait on someone I would complain they weren't on time.

"Hijo, you're Mexican. Act like it," He would say while I would wince about the time. I'd been sitting here in the hotel bar, as nice as it was, for the last thirty minutes and I'd flown a long way for this meeting. I didn't expect to be kept waiting. I didn't even know who I was waiting for. She knew who I was because I had a white rose in my lapel pocket. I felt as if I was on some cheap blind date, the typical bar setting, sipping on a glass of wine, even though it was a little early in the day for drinking it. With the sea breeze and the atmosphere, I couldn't help but indulge myself in the beauty of it all. I even gave Juan some time to enjoy himself. He looked a little lost as I suggested he go do something, but then he grabbed his bag a few minutes later and it was clear he was heading to the gym. I would have joined him, if she'd turned up to the meeting on time. I hadn't come all this way to be stood up.

I was about to get up when the waitress who served me as I had come in, and had spent most of her time observing me, came back with another glass of red wine.

"I didn't order another one. I'm leaving."

She shook her head, "No, sir. Try this one, it's much better than the last one."

They were supposed to bring the bottle and then pour the glass in front of you. I'd been to Italy and Spain enough times to know they had the same customs in bars and restaurants. Yet, she kept coming over with a glass. I was about to complain when I noticed there was a piece of paper underneath the glass. She wasn't only my waitress, but she was the one I was meeting. I smiled at her, and dipped my head discreetly, ready for her to leave the table. Then I looked around and then read her note.

Go to the back in twenty minutes!

I felt naive as if this was my first gig. I should have known it was the waitress. I'd completely let all my guards and senses down. From the moment I stepped in here, she'd been looking at me, as if she knew me. I assumed it was this red suit. Juan did say it was a little too bright. It was suede and besides, just because the sun was out, didn't mean it wasn't cold, so I brought my one suit I could wear while sitting outside and not feel as if my balls were about to drop off. I had a red and brown version of it too, but I'd packed in a hurry and I wasn't worried about what I was going to wear, but more about what I was going to achieve on this trip.

She gave me a drink, without me ordering.

She'd only waited on my table.

Fuck, no wonder I couldn't find Pa's killer, I'd lost all sense of intuition, even when it came to basic things like meeting people and figuring out who they were, instead of the other way around.

I watched my Rolex attentively, while sipping on the wine, waiting eagerly for the twenty minutes to be up. As soon as the time ticked eighteen minutes, I didn't hesitate in getting up, after calculating it would take me two minutes to figure it out and get to the back. I hesitated as I had the last sip of the wine and agreed it had tasted a lot better than the first one, but I hadn't flown thousands of miles to taste the wine.

As I reached the back, she was standing there. No more did she have long dark black hair, or wear square-framed glasses, with the black shirt and pants all the servers wore. Now, she had blonde hair with sunglasses. She kind of reminded me of a female version of Brad Pitt in *Fight Club*. She was smoking and tapping her feet as if I'd been late. I didn't say a word until I strode up to her, taking my time and trying to keep my annoyance at having to wait so long for her to introduce herself. It'd been close to thirty minutes from our original appointment time.

"Are you Vedova Nera?" I asked, but I knew it was a stupid question. She was the Black Widow. The one I needed to help find Pa's killer.

She nodded her head and said, "Now tell me what you need, and I'll see if I can help you."

16

V eronica

I SIGHED as I played around with my food. Friday had come and gone and still no Ricardo. It was as if I was missing him, which seemed weird because I didn't know him and he was the reason I was here. The brief time we'd spent together, he'd turned me on and scared me at the same time, so maybe this was why I was so intrigued by him. No one had ever had this effect on me. Never in my life, but then again, I'd never met a mobster up close and personal until now.

"You should go, go explore the grounds all day. I don't know why you stay inside like an injured dog," Lourdes said, the only one person who did speak to me in the house as I sat down for breakfast. She had a way of making me feel good and bad at the same time. She reminded me of my Aunt Brenda, my dad's sister-in-law. We used to see her all the time as kids, but then as soon as dad left, her appearance in my life did, too. They even dressed alike, flamboyant, as if they were always going to a party. Lourdes had a cute blond bob and I'd seen her when she left the house to go out with her husband last night. They invited me to go along, but three is a crowd. Her husband works on the grounds here, and I could tell when his wife was in her little black short number, he was more than happy I didn't want to come along. I had a feeling they skipped dinner and probably went to a hotel or something because she's tired and has shadows under her eyes as if she's been up all night long. Also, this morning as I was trying to find the kitchen, and bumped into her. She was wearing the same dress as she was last night.

In the house, she appeared to be the perfect housekeeper in her black and white lined uniform dress, but after seeing her last night, I could tell there was a different side to her.

A fun side.

"Wow, you're comparing me to a dog?"

She laughed. "Sometimes, my English is not too good."

Seemed perfect to me!

"I mean, you can go out; you don't have to stay indoors waiting for Mr. Ruiz all day, every day. He'll come soon; besides if you want to know when he's coming then you could call him. I did and he told me," she said as she smiled at me and left the table, probably getting ready to give me a plate full of Mexican eggs. She really wasn't joking when she said that they were something special. That was an understatement; they were delicious. She knew how to cook, and I had to admit that being cooked for was nice, not even the same as going to a restaurant.

I jumped up to follow her. "When is he coming?"

She laughed. "If I tell you. You go outside?"

I moved my head up and down frequently, like the dog, she accused me of being as I smiled at her.

"Okay. He comes on Sunday. So, you have two days to go outside and enjoy the grounds. They are absolutely beautiful and *mi marido* makes sure they are exceptional all the time. Every last flower and every piece of grass."

I agreed. "He does a good job. It's fantastic out there, and the way that you are spoiling me with all your fantastic dishes, I need to exercise a bit. I could have done with losing a few pounds before I arrive, but now I'm sure it's a lot more."

She giggled. "There's nothing better than a man having something to grab a hold of."

I giggled like a teenager, as she put her hands on her hips, and swung them around. Mainly, because she was so petite, I couldn't think what part of her body she was referring to, there was no meat on her.

"How do you know about the grounds?"

I shrugged. "I see them from the window."

She laughed. "It's not the same as standing in it. Feeling the grass in between your feet, smelling the flowers. You need to go outside."

She was right, I was indoors, scared of my future and worried about what he was going to do to me. Yet, here I was, eagerly awaiting his return.

"I'm going to finish my coffee and *mis huevos* and then I'm out of here."

She smiled at me, and I thought she would say something about my pronunciation, but she said nothing as she continued working. I could go out, take some photos, and send them to Jen. It would put her mind at ease, knowing that things weren't so bad. Besides, they were far from that. I had Lourdes as company, and not only was she friendly, but she was a fantastic cook.

17

R icardo

I WAS SITTING in a strip bar, and judging by the look on Juan's
face, he was enjoying it a lot more than I was; he was paying
more attention to the girls than he was to whether anyone was
about to attack me. Then again, he wasn't exactly my body-
guard and I could handle myself.

One thing for sure, it was a mixed crowd, the Italians seated
together, well dressed and stylish. The rest were a mix of Brits,
Americans and even a couple of Mexicans. We nodded at each
other as I entered, as if to acknowledge we were one and the
same. I wasn't a regular participant at strip clubs. They were
one of the few places men seemed to lose their minds and
became targets used as a weapon against their enemy. Hits were
frequent at clubs like this, places they knew their enemies were
feeble and they could take full opportunity of the situation.

This was the real reason I hated the place, and why I didn't feel at ease.

I felt fucking weak.

"Mierda!" I blurted out, as some man nearly tripped over my feet as he took a stripper to the back. He didn't even apologize, and I did my best to keep my cool, thinking if the girl didn't turn up soon, I would count this trip a loss. I couldn't be bothered to have the run around anymore. She told me to meet her at the bar. I did. Then I waited and met her at the back. I told her I was trying to find Pa's killer and she told me to wait here until Saturday and meet her at this club. I don't like being told what to do, it was bad enough waiting, let alone coming here.

"The main attraction for the night. The one. The only. Medusa!" The MC said in both English and Italian. The lights dimmed and she had everyone's attention, as the lights flashed gold and black. I was intrigued by what the main attraction had to offer, as she had turned the loud bar into a quiet one.

The wall at the back turned black with gold studs, the one pole was in the center became the main attraction and a woman dressed in a silver jacket with a matching hat walked onto the stage. She circled the pole, not revealing her face or her body, and the crowd went wild. Until she started to strip and like famished wolves ready to catch her jacket and hat, they had their hands up ready to please.

Her full-sized breasts were held together by two strings, one could call a bikini, but I thought of it as nothing but strings, as for her panties, again one gold strip that was from her front to her back. Nothing about her outfit left anything to anyone's imagination about her body. Everything was on display, then she lifted one leg in the air, to reveal .her pussy was clean-shaven. The men went wild as they all stood and threw money at her. It wasn't until she swayed her hips from left-to-right that I realized she was the waitress, the Vedova Nera. The reason I was here tonight. No more did I feel anxious about it all, but instead a little horny. I looked to my left and realized even Juan was taken in by her beauty or maybe it was her pussy, breasts, or the whole fucking package. It was as if she hypnotized us all as she elegantly swayed on the pole, doing splits, laying on the floor, her legs wide open for all to admire. Her string sometimes moved, revealing her nipples which were hard and erect.

I couldn't help but adjust in my seat, as I watched the woman who I was going to hire to help find my Pa's killer move naturally on the pole. She seductively moved around it, as if she was born to do it. As if she'd been giving lessons from day one, not taking them. Her eyes met mine, and I didn't shy away from them. I could have pretended, but I didn't as I slipped my hand in my jacket and followed suit and threw Euros at her. I didn't know how many I had in my hand or the value of them all. As soon as I'd done enough, she moved away from me and crawled to the other side of the stage. I watched her twerk her butt away from me as if she was rewarding me for the money I'd given her. I didn't sit down, I couldn't as I watched her twerk not only her butt but even her breasts. The strings that had held them firm against her body were broken as she did, and her nipples. God, they were so hard; not only was she turning every man on who was watching her, it was as if she was getting off on it too and she wanted us all to know.

I loved and hated her because I had my own toy waiting for me back home and I didn't want to spoil my plans with her, the desire to have another woman, wouldn't make my experience with Veronica memorable and I didn't want anything to ruin it. So, I backed away as if I'd been woken up from the spell that she'd put on us. I turned my back and drank my drink. I ignored the crowds, the noises of the bar as I started to head out.

"Jefe, I think the best bit's coming."

I dipped my head at him, encouraged him to watch the rest of the show.

I came to Sicily to find Pa's killer, not to have wine and certainly not to watch a strip show. I could have watched it back home, privately in the comfort of my own home, and for free. I didn't have to take a jet to fly to risky territories. This whole place could be a trap. I started to leave, feeling silly for coming here and thinking this could be the answer to my question.

"Mr. Ruiz, Vedova Nera would like to see you in her room," a goon said as he grabbed hold of my arm. I shook off his hand, and he moved it as if he'd done nothing wrong. I followed him, thinking... I wondered if she'd known I would leave. I wondered if she'd planned everything down to the last second. I smiled, as I realized, she was good, and exactly who I needed to find Pa's killer.

I SAT SIPPING THE WINE, the same one I'd drank at the bar had been waiting for me in her room. She had what I could only imagine to be every stripper's changing room. There were a ton of wigs, bikinis, dresses all hanging up, in different sections around the room. This wasn't the part which caught my eye, though; it was the photos on the wall. I'd seen and met some of my relatives, and even the dead ones were still respected, and their photos hung up on the walls of our houses. Tio David, Jorge and Fern, and then there were photos of famous stars, Al Pacino, De Vito, etc.

Who the fuck was she?

How old was she?

Tio David was well into his seventies, but he looked as if he was in his forties in this photo. But the stripper and waitress I'd met, couldn't have been more than thirty. Judging by these photos, you would think they had only been taken yesterday because she looks the same.

"It's rude to leave a show, before it ends," Vedova Nera

slurred as she entered the room. I didn't even hear her entered, she startled me, and the glass of wine in my hand, nearly went crashing to the floor.

"I think it's even ruder to leave someone waiting for thirty minutes before you identify yourself and request an extra three days. I have a feeling you've wasted my time," I concluded as I slammed the glass on the table and moved toward the door. The door Vedova Nera stood in front of.

"I see. So, waiting annoyed you."

She shut the door. The lighting was dim in her room, like the club. Then again, it needed to have a certain amount of atmosphere to it. It was a strip club, not a fucking shopping mall. The dim light needed to hide all the flaws, like maybe it wasn't her in the same foto with Tio David. Maybe my mind was playing tricks on me again.

"Does my nakedness bother you?" Vedova Nera asked as she drew closer.

"Not as much as your tardiness."

She was so close I could feel her breasts pressed against my chest, so I backed away. I didn't want to lose control, as much as she was tempting me. I needed to go home. I had work to do and so far, all I'd done over the last few days was focus on Pa's killer. I hadn't even bothered with anything else, and Vedova Nera was wasting my time. I had to get the fuck out of here before I did something I would regret.

"You're not like most men, Ricardo. Some would have left the moment they arrived at the bar. Others would have tried to fuck me from the moment they saw me on stage. You. You want revenge so badly, nothing else will do."

I dipped my head. "Exactly. So, are you going to help me or are you going to keep wasting my time?"

"Did you find a girl?" Vedova Nera asked casually as if she was talking about me running an errand for her and as if it would be so easy. Well, it had been, but she didn't need to know.

"Yes."

Vedova Nera paused as she headed to the mirror, no doubt to touch-up her make-up.

"She knows nothing of your plan."

"Nothing."

She nodded again as if she was satisfied with my answers. Then she moved away from me and headed to the mirror and chair which took up most of the space in her room.

"Well, as I said to you on the phone, you keep her happy. When I'm ready for her, I'll send for her."

"We could have had this conversation on the phone. She's already been at my house for nearly five days."

I was pissed, not so much at Vedova Nera, but at myself. She'd told me to get an innocent before my trip. Veronica crashed into me, and then saved me from having to look for someone. It was as if fate drew her to me.

Vedova Nera agreed. "We could have, but then I wouldn't be doing what you ask. I need to see all my clients personally. See them. Figure out what they're like before agreeing to work for them. I can't work for just anyone; I have a reputation to keep. A good one at that, otherwise, you wouldn't be here. You know all about reputations, don't you? They're important in this line of work."

I was confused about the last statement; we were not in the same business.

"But you'll strip for anyone. Besides we're not in the same business."

She laughed. "You think you know me, Ruiz. You think because I strip, you're better than me."

I shook my head. "I don't. But, I didn't hire you to get acquainted with you. I hired you to help find my father's killer. I never knew you knew my family. You have some of my uncles on your wall."

"No. That's my mum. Not me. I'm not that old. Ruiz, do what you will; you came here because you have failed. Because you couldn't find your father's killer. I don't owe you anything," she purred as she moved from her seat to face me, backing me against her wall.

I knew exactly what she was doing, I'd insulted Vedova Nera so she was returning the favor. She was right; it felt as if venom had left her mouth.

"Seeing as we're on the same page. I expect to have results." I turned around and faced the door, turned the handle and stepped out.

Diego and Lourdes had been looking after Veronica and making her feel like a guest in the house. If Veronica thought she should be scared of me, she was wrong. The person she should be scared of was Vedova Nera, the one I'd just left behind in her changing room. Vedova Nera was the one who was pissed right now, and I had a feeling she was disappointed I'd never made an advance on her. Knowing my uncles, they'd already had a slice of Vedova Nera and her mother's pie, more than enough times. I didn't want to go down any road my uncles had been down, I didn't care who she was, I was paying her five million to catch Pa's killer. I wasn't interested in anything else she had to offer. As I finally made it outside, I was shocked to see Juan outside waiting for me. For some reason, I thought he had been enjoying himself a little too much inside there, and like all men who get lost in the strip club, he would forget to find his way back out.

"Jefe, listo?" he asked with a big smile on his face, which made me realize he had been enjoying himself in there.

"Yeah, let's go home. I don't want to go back to the hotel. I want to get out of here and back home, now."

His face dropped; maybe he had plans for tonight. He had

to cancel. I had plans of my own and none of them involved staying in Sicily another night. She seemed to know what she was doing, even though I hated to be tested. I needed to wait for her to contact me, and not the other way around. If I failed her test in any way, I would be joining Pa in the fridge.

18

eronica

I WAS bored and tired at the same time. I'd spent all my life working, I wasn't used to sitting back and doing nothing. I asked Lourdes if I could help her prepare dinner in exchange for her sitting down with me at lunch this afternoon. She was reluctant, but I smiled and she agreed; she claimed I had an irresistible smile. For the first time in my life, I realized how lonely I was; the only person I went out with socially was Jen. None of the other girls tried to socialize with me outside of work. Then again, the feeling was mutual. We didn't have anything in common outside of work because I did nothing else but work.

When did I get so boring?

I didn't listen to music anymore. I couldn't remember the last time I had a favorite tune?

Or even a favorite book?

I had even given up my twice-weekly sessions of yoga, so I could work even longer hours. How could anyone socialize with someone who lived in their own bubble?

"If I knew helping me in the kitchen would make you so sad, I would have said no," Lourdes said, bringing me back down to reality.

"Remember the other day, you told me to go and explore the grounds, and there's a library, I can go read a book, or even go to the gym and workout or go to the movie theatre downstairs and watch a movie."

She nodded her head in confirmation, as I stated what she already knew about the house.

"Well, I realized, I could do all these things back home. And I do none of them."

She laughed. "How old are you? You're too young to not have a life."

"Twenty-four."

"Arrh, I remember being young. I used to do so much, maybe too much." She laughed, probably remembering all the things she used to get up to. Then she shook her head. "What do you like to do?"

As if we were talking about me, and not her.

I laughed. "Work."

"What do you do in your free time?"

"Get ready to go to work."

"On the weekend?" She put the pot down, ready for me to say something other than work, but she was wrong as I said. "Work."

She started to count with her fingers. "You have no hobbies, no boyfriend, no social life, please tell me that you have friends?"

"One," I blurted out.

Then she turned around and smiled. "I don't know what to

say to you. Everyone's different; doesn't mean it has to be bad, just different. Right, are you ready to make paella?"

I put on the apron and said, "Maybe if I learn this well then he'll keep me so I can make him paella."

She laughed. "There's no way you can make paella as good as me."

"Bring it on. Let's see."

Her smile turned into a frown as she started to talk, about the way I needed to wash my hands and the order of the ingredients. I should have saved all the instructions on my phone, as I realized she was right. There was no way I was going to make paella as good as her, and I was clearly kidding myself as she told me it took her years to perfect her skills.

Then again, as we just had established, time was something I had plenty of, all the time.

19

R icardo

FINALLY, I made it home. I told Lourdes what time I would arrive, and she told me dinner was ready and waiting for me in the dining room as Juan parked the car. As he came to a stop in the driveway, I remembered I had company. The whole flight the only thing on my mind was Vedova. Why was she playing on my mind when I had Veronica waiting for me? I hated the way Vedova had treated me, like a little boy on the playground who needed direction from her to know how to play. No, I didn't need direction from anyone, especially the likes of her.

"Jefe, you want me to stick around?"

"No, go home. Get some rest."

He smiled. "Sure thing."

That kind of surprised me, Juan seemed a little disappointed when I told him we were leaving, yet he was quite happy once we did arrive back. As I opened the car door he asked, "Jefe, como estas?"

I didn't answer him as I sat up and stepped out of the car. I needed to have a shot of something and go to bed; no more did I feel the need to eat, as we came back in the Range Rover and not the limo. At least I could have had a few shots in the back, but there was nothing in the Rover and I was dying for a drink.

"Bien!" I deliberated as I slammed the door shut and thought about which one to tackle first, a Remy Martin or Armagnac?

I waved, then walked up to the front door. As soon as I opened the front door, I was in fucking shock. There were candles on the floor, and it didn't take a fucking genius to figure out they were leading to the dining room. I shut the door, and then the candles went out near the door. I followed them, every stride I took with haste as it made me even madder. It could have been the lack of sleep or even Vedova. Either way, when I reached the dining room and Veronica faced me in an off-the-shoulder red ball gown dress, her hair tied up loosely, her breasts on full display, it awoke a lion inside of me and one she wasn't prepared to meet.

"Mierda!" I blurted as I reached closer to her. She was shaking, the same way she had been when I got the ax out of the car.

I needed her to be afraid of me, and not to think of me as some romantic gesture; otherwise, nothing would work nor go according to plan.

"What did I do?" She cried, her glass dropping to the floor as she stood.

"What is all this? Lourdes told me dinner was ready, but what are you—all dressed up as dessert?"

It was cruel. I wanted her to be comfortable, but not to think of us as some romantic notion. I wanted to play with her, when I felt the need, but nothing more. Diego was the one I was really pissed off with, but he wasn't here, and unfortunately, my fury was taken out on her as a result of it.

"You told me to make myself at home."

I choked. "It seems as if you've done a lot more than that. I said make yourself comfortable, this is fucking different. We've hardly met and here you are dressing yourself up for the night's events. We're not married. We're not even going out; what the fuck were you thinking?"

I grabbed her hand, and barked, "Come with me!" I was taking her to the room, the one where I took anyone who crossed me, but I didn't want them to die a quick death. No, rather a long and painful one.

"What did I do wrong? You're hurting me?" She was crying and trying to keep up the pace but struggling with her heels.

I stopped and yanked them off, throwing them to the side.

"Now you can walk properly. I told you that you were the price for hitting my car."

She didn't say a word; maybe the shock of it all had made her go into silent mode, which was good for me. I knew I was being cruel, but she had to learn her fucking place.

I was chanting while I was walking, but she was struggling to keep up. Maybe Lourdes had been overfeeding her; it wouldn't surprise me. She did get bored cooking for me alone, and when the gang came over, she would always cook for a whole army. She was a natural in the kitchen.

"If I wanted someone to fuck, then I would have done it in Sicily. I wouldn't have gone to the expense of getting you a new closet. If I wanted a girlfriend, then I wouldn't have told you to stay here for thirty days in exchange for a place by my side. I would have come to get you every day, not flown to Italy and made sure you waited here for me. Some people have known me for years; they know where my house is, but I would never let them step inside it," I stopped making sure she was paying attention. She was whimpering and her once green eyes were now brown. She wore contacts. Her eyes were fake. I flashed my eyes over her body, wondering what else about her was fake.

I continued as we headed to the dungeons. "If I wanted a wife, then I would have gone back home to my Mexican village. I would make sure she didn't speak English and knew nothing about American life. Hell, no. I would want her to cook, clean, and be a dutiful wife. I told you to come here for none of the three. So, any romantic gesture or notion in your head, you better fucking get them out."

I told Diego and he knew, I wanted her settled in the house so she wouldn't be bored, there was nothing worse than an idle woman. But somewhere in the midst of things, he'd given her the idea this was a *Pretty Woman* scenario. I was pissed with him, but he wasn't around, and the only one I could take my anger on was her. I'd taken Veronica from the streets and turned her into some kind of princess. No, life wasn't like the movies, especially in my world. Any woman I did take from the streets and make them into a princess would have to be Mexican and would have to be properly vetted. Not just her, but her whole damn family, including the family pet.

"Here," I said as I unlocked the door to go down the stairs. We started to climb down the stairs and she was not walking willingly anymore. I had to stop, as she refused to go on, and then she screamed, "Where are you taking me?"

She didn't wait for a reply as she started to cry, as I lifted her to my shoulder and I think she bumped her head a bit. The dungeon was colder, a lot colder than I remembered, but she would survive. Maybe one night or two. I continued down the stairs, she felt a lot heavier than I imagined; which meant Lourdes had definitely been overfeeding her. The light flickered against the brick wall as we arrived at the cage. By now, she was kicking her feet against me and screaming. I'd had it built for more than one person. I opened the door, trying to steady myself at the same time, and get away from her screams which were becoming deafening because they were echoing off the walls.

"Let me go! This is kidnapping! You can't leave me here for twenty-five days, I'll die."

Oh, so she'd been counting the days while she'd been in the house.

I opened the cage and tossed her inside, by the time she realized what was happening and ran to the door, it locked. It self-locked and I left her whimpering and crying because my back was hurting. She was strong, and a fighter, I would give her that. But she was no match for me. By this time tomorrow, she wouldn't have the energy to fight. I might even leave her down there another day, so she knows her place.

I ignored her screams and curses as I remembered seeing black paella on the table before I grabbed her. Lourdes had made my favorite dish and I was starving. Tomorrow I would have to deal with Diego, realistically, I should put him in the dungeon, too. He'd given Veronica the wrong idea, a mistake unfortunately, she was paying the price for right now.

She helped make up my mind as I reached the top of the stairs, I needed a Remy Martin to go with my meal. Maybe I would just have a shot of Armagnac before I hit the sack.

DIEGO WALKED INTO THE LIBRARY. I'd called for him to be here at seven this morning. He arrived five minutes earlier to make sure he was in the library on time. I looked up at the antique clock hung on the wall as he walked in.

"Primo, you're back in one piece. Do you feel better, do you..."

I didn't give him the same greeting, as I didn't mess around, and got to business.

"I told you to make sure Veronica was made comfortable, not Lady of the Manor."

His smile turned to a frown. Like all members of our family, we didn't like to be criticized and prided ourselves on getting everything right. A job well done is something to be proud of; a job not done well, usually meant you would be buried in the backyard earlier than your time.

"You said to make her comfortable. I did. Anything else would have meant making her sleep with the dogs in the kennel," he said in his defense. I didn't offer him a seat, and I could tell by the way he was wound up, he wasn't in the mood to sit with me, either.

"It's called common sense. I told you I needed her to help me find Pa's killer, which didn't mean I want her to be a lady of the night or even day."

"Lo siento. I thought you would want a piece of ass. She has a hot ass, and you really need for things to go back to the way they were before."

I loosened up, as Diego always had a way of making me laugh.

"She does, especially seeing as Lourdes has been feeding her well."

He shook his head. "Primo, you're too wound up these days. I think she could be exactly what you need, you get me?"

I sighed. "I do, but I don't want her getting the wrong idea, and last night she really had the wrong idea. Time's running out and I don't know when I'll need her."

"How did Italy go?" He changed the subject as he headed to the bar at the corner of the library. Sometimes, I needed an early morning wake-up call, and judging by the look on his face, he hadn't gotten much sleep between the message I sent him six hours ago and him arriving here now. He had been worried he'd done something wrong and he had, but didn't know what until now. He was probably relieved it wasn't as bad as he thought it would be. I had been in his shoes once or twice, too many times with Pa.

He didn't wait for me to reply as he said, "Wait. Where is she?"

Then he took his shot, probably his relief shot. He glanced at my glass as if to say I didn't need a refill. No, I didn't, I'd drank a little too much before going to bed and eating. Then a little more this morning, I didn't need any more for now, but I still kept it close.

"Downstairs."

I moved my head to the side, waiting for his reaction. There wasn't any and he didn't even bother asking if I meant the wine cellar or the dungeon because he knew exactly which part she was being held in.

"I see. So, you want me to take care of her?" He asked, standing by my side with his eyebrow raised.

"Exactly."

"For how long?" He asked, probably wondering how he would fit that in with everything else he had going on at the moment.

"Until tomorrow evening, and then we're done."

"Good," he shot back and then he left without saying another word, I didn't have to spell it out to him, he knew she was in the dungeon, all he had to do was make sure she survived. Afterward, Veronica would be my responsibility once again. His mom was a nurse and he'd learned so much from her. Diego would make sure she was fed, warm, and had anything else she needed while she was down there. I had other things to deal with, like finding who had been taking money out of my account. You give people an inch and they take a whole fucking mile. The war had already begun; the word was out that I still hadn't found Pa's killer, so they were fucking with me. It was working, I had to find out not only who killed Pa, but who was after me, too.

20

eronica

I WAS TIRED, wet and cold. I didn't know what the time was, or even the day. With what little strength I had in me, I ripped my dress, so the part below my knee was covering my bare shoulders as I laid on the stone ground. The only light in this cave, was when Ricardo was here; as soon as he'd left, I'd had all of five seconds to take in my surroundings to know everywhere was brick, including the floor. It was cold and damp, and there was a bucket at the side of the wall. One I assumed was for me to urinate or even shit in. I wanted to so badly, so the next time Ricardo came in here, I would throw it at him.

How dare he?

I crashed into his fucking car, and he treats me like this!

He might as well have killed me, it would have been better than this, anything would have been. I was dying to pee, so I crawled because I couldn't walk. Nearly every part of my body was hurting me. I had been drinking so much wine out of nerves before he arrived, that I had been slightly light-headed when he came through the door. I didn't realize at first that he was angry, I thought he was excited. Boy, was I wrong.

I tried moving on the brick floor, but it scratched my body and now my stomach was hurting from the hunger. I knew it was only a matter of time before he gave me food, or did he plan on leaving me here to rot and starve, all because I cooked a nice meal for him with Lourdes and dressed up.

What a fucking monster.

What would he have done with me, if I'd gone all out and laid on the table in my breakfast suit? There was nothing attractive about him. I hated him, and to think I had simply misunderstood the situation, so his answer for it all was to punish me. If I did survive this, then I'd return the favor, there would be no doubt about it.

One good thing was at least the bucket was clean. I stopped in my tracks as I reached for it, and then slowly tried to stand-up, there wasn't a muscle or even a piece of fat on my body which wasn't hurting, as I tried to stand up. Then, I pulled down my panties, and I couldn't believe they were glued to me, so much so I had trouble pulling them down. I was stiff as I bent down, I couldn't even stoop as I tried, but then I flopped my ass on the bucket and peed. I didn't care that there was nothing to wash my hands with, or even paper to wipe myself down after. I let it all come flowing out. I sighed as I put my head back, happy simply that the steel bucket didn't crash or lose balance with my weight. As I came to an end, I quickly stood, then used the bottom of my knickers to soak up the remaining drops of my urine. I could have used the part of the dress I ripped off, but it was the one thing which was keeping me warm, and I couldn't have it soaked with urine. I had to improvise, but I could just about see, as there was a thin streak of light coming into the cave. It let me know where the bucket was, but the rest of the cave was a mystery to me. I felt like a blind woman, as I couldn't see past the bucket, and I couldn't even retrace my steps back to where I had been sleeping, but I couldn't stay here any longer. I had to move away. The smell of my urine filled not only my nose, but the cave too, so I moved away, back into the darkness, trying not to think about what I'd done as my stomach started to make noises I'd never heard before.

Then, all of a sudden, there was light again. It felt as if Christmas had come early. I didn't want to show the fear, the anger I was feeling deep down inside of me, in case by some miracle Ricardo had realized the error of his ways and decided to set me free. Maybe he did have a heart after all.

I couldn't make out who it was, the sound of the steps, and the bright light made me turn blind, it was too bright. I didn't remember it being bright earlier, but maybe after being in the dark so long, it'd hurt my eyes. No one spoke, I couldn't bring myself to do it, as I huddled into a corner, and waited for someone to speak as I closed my eyes.

"Hey, Veronica, it's me, Diego."

I dipped my head my head, surprised to hear his voice, but I didn't feel like small talk right now. The humiliation of it all was too much to bear.

"Ricardo's pissed, but it's my fault. I should have briefed you and done things differently."

I cried, "What? You should have put me in here, first."

"No. ...it doesn't matter. The good news is I can get you out tomorrow. The bad news is you have one more night here. So, I brought blankets. I'll clean the bucket, and I brought wipes and..."

"Food, did you bring food?"

"Yeah, bread and water. But it's for one more night."

"Oh," I said as I jumped up, and then with the blinding light and using my hands as a navigator, I managed to find my way to him. I didn't hesitate in taking the bread and water from him. He'd let himself in the cage and was standing in front of me. I could have made a run for it, I could have tried, but I knew if I did then Ricardo was probably somewhere watching, and he would definitely kill me. There would be no hesitation, I had to play along, as Diego had said for one more night.

I felt sick at the idea of eating, without washing my hands, but I was too voracious to care about hygiene. It all seemed relative. I was being held like an animal, and the last thing on my mind should have been about not acting like one.

"So, I'm leaving the paper, food on this side, and then the bucket on the other side. I've got a fresh one. I'll change then I'll be back in the morning to change it and by then get you out of here."

I should have said thanks, but I had a feeling he didn't want my gratitude. He wasn't facing me when he was talking, but the side of the wall. Strange.

"Right, let's get the bucket changed."

He paused as if he was waiting for something, I looked at the bottle of water, the two-liter bottle, and the loaf of fresh bread he'd laid in the corner, with new clothes and blankets. At least I wouldn't be as cold as I was last night.

"What time is it?"

"One," he said and nodded. "In the afternoon."

Shit, I'd been here for only one night and afternoon, yet it felt like an eternity.

"I'll let you out tomorrow morning."

"What time?"

It felt silly worrying about the time when I had nowhere to go. I couldn't be let out, even fucking criminals who were incarcerated were treated better than this.

"He'll let me know," he pointed to the top of the cell and this was when I realized what he was talking to seconds ago. The camera. This is why it was so bright in here, the camera was shining and checking every part of this hell. This is why earlier when I wanted to pee, he must have activated the light to guide me along. Fuck! I really hated him now.

I slumped back into the corner, the one where Diego had left the blankets and new clothes for me. Knowing I was being watched made me hesitate for a split second before getting changed. I'd lost all self-esteem from the moment I was put in this cell. Diego backed away, probably embarrassed by the fact I was stripping in front of him. Every part of my body stunk, from my urinated panties to my teeth. Ricardo had stripped me of all dignity and I hated him, and I wished I hadn't crashed into his car.

I wished I had crashed directly into him.

21

R icardo

I WATCHED as she stripped and changed in front of Diego. I could have set her free, seeing as she'd realized the error of her ways, and let her go to her room. The one she was given on the first day she stayed here—but I had no intention of letting her go back to the room as it was. I made Lourdes strip the handmade Turkish rug, the queen-sized bed, all clothes, toiletries, and furniture from the room. She would only have wooden floors and a small single bed. Nothing more. She'd have to wear the same thing every day: black leggings and a matching shirt. She wouldn't be attractive to herself, let alone me. No television. No access to Wi-Fi. Nothing. She would feel like a prisoner, until the day came when she would be allowed to go out, and she would obey knowing if she rebelled then her fate would be one of two options: death or the dungeon. She would welcome both with open arms.

After her twenty-three days were up, then she could go on with her life, pretending she had never met me, or that I'd done nothing but treat her well. If all went well, her bank account would have money she would never have imagined possible in her wildest dreams. Maybe by then I would be gone, whoever I was seeking would pay my revenge price, and then the circle of the mob life would continue until eventually, we'd all be beyond the grave or behind bars.

"Did you need me today, jefe?" Juan asked as he entered the library. I shook my head as I watched Veronica on my phone. She was lying down in the same corner, not wanting to eat again, but just sleep. I knew she had nothing but regret on her mind, regret for crashing her car into me, regret for coming to this house. I stirred the Remy Martin I had poured into my glass as I watched her. I was so fascinated by her I even forgot Juan was in the room.

"I`ll be on my way, and I'll be back on Friday."

I dipped my head. I knew where he was going. He'd brought the girl, the one he met in Sicily, and he planned to show her around town. It was crazy to think someone like Juan believed in love at first sight. The next day, he had told me he wanted her here. I told him to do what he liked, not my business. Apparently, he met her in the gym, and they seemed to hit it off straight away. Jose told me his brother was acting like a little baby, claiming he was in love. I didn't care, I wanted revenge. What Juan did with his time was his business.

"Remember, you have the meeting in ten minutes."

My eyes shot at him. I didn't need a secretary, let alone Juan telling me what I needed to do.

"Chao!" he said as he turned red, embarrassed by his statement. I was going to have a tough meeting with the gang, which was why I needed a stiff drink.

I stood, ready to face the music. Today wasn't going to be pretty. I felt bad about putting Veronica in the dungeon, but minutes ago Vendova had told me to have Veronica ready in five days. I needed Veronica to be prepared for whatever Vendova was going to throw at her. I decided keeping her in the dungeon one day longer would do the trick.

I walked into the conference room at the back of the house. Someone was stealing from me, and I didn't want Juan to get wind of there being an issue among the top five. One thing was for certain; it wasn't Juan. I knew there was a possibility it was Jose, but I couldn't think about what he had to gain from stealing. He wasn't a man who loved the finer things in life. I couldn't imagine him using the money to buy a fancy suit or sports car. He drove a beat-up Renault, pretty much what Veronica had driven before it was completely written off. No, he wasn't an option, but I wanted him to be present at this meeting, to know there was a problem.

Diego was a prime candidate until I had seen the way he treated Veronica a few minutes ago. He showed acts of kindness, but he didn't go behind my back and try and set her free. He could have done as much, but he hadn't from the time I told him to go to her this morning. He waited until now to do it, showing me his loyalty. Which left Frank, who was an outsider, who had joined us only three months ago. I didn't know who Tom Hardy was until Marta described he reminded her of him, with his British accent and bad boy of the London street appearance.

We needed someone new. Someone who others didn't know and most of all wasn't Mexican. It was a strategy we'd tried and tested for years, and unfortunately, one foreigner would always get hit first, which was another reason why we did it. If someone wanted to hit us back, they would pop the outsider first; if they wanted to start a war, they would pop one of the family members.

Or it could leave Marta, the one woman on our team. She was my cousin, so far down the line, I didn't have enough fingers to count how far down the family chain we were related, but she was good at what she did, from seducing politicians, to being a cat burglar. She clearly was an obvious choice, but she was family, and she knew the rule: don't steal from family. Then again, not everyone lived by the rules. Especially with fucking technology and the way the world was going mad. Jose was even showing me a way we could kill people online. Imagine, what the fuck is the fun in that? Pressing a button and having something take away all the glory. I nearly died laughing when he suggested it, he didn't understand the business if he thought killing people online was a way forward. Maybe the next generation, but not in mine.

Jose said it could be simple, by taking every penny out of someone's account, leaving them penniless; making them think their loved ones have been cheating on them by posting false pictures on social media; and Jose's personal favorite, social bullying. The final act worked a lot better than the others, so I'd been told by Jose.

Triggers that would result in some, not all committing suicide. Society was weak, and social humiliation had become the trigger to killing someone, instead of physically harming them.

I went to the back of the house. I could usually jog down here, but for some reason, even walking had taken all the energy out of me. I was exhausted and couldn't think what else to do but slow down my heart rate so I didn't burst into flames like I had last night. I went back to the library to grab a bottle, but the Remy Martin was empty, which meant not only was someone stealing money from my account, but they were drinking my expensive shit, too.

I opened the doors with both hands and everyone was talking like they always did whenever we got together. I was still grieving, missing the old man. Coming to terms with him not being around didn't allow me to plan the usual social events. A dinner. A barbecue. A party. Nah, wouldn't be done for a long time.

Frank stood as I arrived; he was a former defender working for a DA.

I needed some parts of my business to be legit, so I had a law firm for my legal dealings, but whenever they hired a new person to deal with a particular case, I would get Frank to look over it. He was good at reviewing the finer details. A case went wrong for him, and instead of moving to the defender side of things, which most prosecutors did in this case, he asked me for a job. He heard I was looking and wanted to work for me. I was dubious at first, but he charmed me. I haven't met a lawyer who wasn't been able to charm someone. The shit ones can't but the good ones like Frank, it just comes fucking naturally.

He sat down, embarrassed about getting up and as usual, Marta laughed as he sat down.

"Primo, como estás?" (Cousin, how are you?)Marta smiled at me, as she walked over to give me kisses on the cheek. I smiled back, but I wasn't in the mood, so I got down to business before anyone else started asking about my trip.

"Fine. Look, I called you here today for a reason."

Jose said, "Yeah, someone's been stealing. Juan told me. Look, it isn't me."

As if I had accused him of stealing straightaway. I turned around and closed the door before the conversation got heated. No one came to this part of the house whenever there was a meeting, Lourdes made sure of it by making sure no staff was in the house. Veronica was here, but there was no way she was going to hear anything we were going to discuss.

"Joder! Did you call us here 'cause you think we been stealing from you primo?" Marta asked, she stood, most likely ready to storm out. She was only five foot two, slim, and in shape. Her blonde hair was tied up and she had on a short black number which left nothing to the imagination. One thing for sure, she may have been short in height, but her personality was so damn strong that she more than made up for it, being the smallest in the room.

"I need to find out who has done it."

I lied; I did think one of them had done it. They were the closest to me, and there was no fucking way Lourdes or Juan would even dream about it, which only left the four of them.

"Fine, I did it," Frank said and then he tilted his head to the side, then he ran his hand through his dark hair and then his blue eyes looked at me as if to challenge me to do something about it.

"Okay," I lifted my arms. They got me.

"I admit, I did think one of you did it. You're the closest to me and no one else has access."

Diego choked out, "You are kidding, I keep telling you, you're too old school. No one needs to be near you to steal from you. All this shit can be done online. Look if you call me here again for this type of shit, then I'm out. I've got shit to do."

"You're not fucking going anywhere," I demanded for him to sit back down. He was acting as if he was in charge, losing his position in this group.

"Jose, tell him, you're the computer genius," Diego asked as he turned his head to Jose.

Jose agreed. "Yeah, Diego's right. If someone's stealing, then it could be a hacker. It doesn't have to do with us being close to you or anything."

Diego stood, ready to leave. Seeing as Jose had confirmed what he'd already suspected in the space of five seconds, I felt like a fool.

"Fuck, don't you fucking move. I called you guys here to find out who's stealing from me. It started two weeks ago, but with Pa gone, I didn't notice. I was going over the businesses today, and this was when I saw it, as clear as day."

Frank agreed, "If it was so fucking clear, then why didn't you notice the one obvious thing."

He'd completely lost me. I shook my head, encouraging him to clarify his statement.

"It most likely happened the day Pa died, which means someone is out to get you. Most likely bring the whole family down. Isn't this how it works?" Frank asked Diego, most likely because Frank was a little older than him and they seemed to be always on the same wavelength, making me feel like the old man. Marta and Frank had a thing once. Frank still felt the same; it was obvious by the way he looked at Marta, but he was wasting his time, Marta was the love them and leave them type. I'd seen her break too many hearts, and the moment she hooked up with Frank, I knew it was a matter of time before she would do the same thing to him.

Diego shrugged. "I guess so. But you must admit, Primo, the fact it started the same time as Pa does seem weird."

Shit, this meant I had to find out what happened to Pa sooner rather than later. Not only did they take him away from me, but they wanted to show me they could mess with me. No, they fucking couldn't and I had to somehow show the same team I accused of stealing from me, that I needed their help.

"When you figure it out, then let us know," Marta said as she stood ready to leave.

"Wait, we need to work together. We need..."

Diego interrupted. "You need to get some sleep. You're getting fucking paranoid..."

Marta said, "Like thinking, we would steal from you. It fucking hurts. Look, get some sleep like D said and then we'll talk tomorrow or the day after when you feel better."

Diego wasn't talking about accusing them of stealing as the issue; he was talking about Veronica and he avoided eye contact as he followed suit and left the room. I should have popped him, then and there since he was out of line.

Frank cleared his throat, stood, and did the same. This left Jose and me in the room. Neither of us spoke as everyone left and the door was closed.

"What do you need me to do?" Jose asked, breaking the ice, as it was clear he was uncomfortable with the way things went down.

"Nada," I said as I got up and left the room, I had nothing to say to Jose. I looked at my phone to make sure Diego hadn't set Veronica free and she was still in the dungeon. I shook my head as I saw her in the same position and realized Diego was right. I was getting paranoid; I'd accused my team of being disloyal to me. I was acting like an old fool. This was the type of thing which made a loyal team unfaithful. I needed to get some rest as Diego said; otherwise, I would have no gang, and I would be alone.

I needed to get my rest and try and be more sensitive to others. Something I'd never done before, but I had to start doing it now.

22

eronica

I'D SLEPT EVER since Diego left the bread and water for me. Whenever I woke up, I forced myself to drift off to sleep again. The idea of having nothing to do and being watched all the time made me think of unpleasant memories. Such as dad leaving, or the way my sisters behaved after the funeral. Or rather, Alice not coming, and Rebecca pretending I didn't exist.

"You didn't eat or drink anything, after I left?" a male voice said.

I was feeling disoriented and for some reason, it took a while for me to realize Diego was talking to me, not mom. For some reason, I was caught between my reality and my subconscious. He'd either come to change the bucket I hadn't used, or he'd come to get me out of here. It was then I smelled it and realized I hadn't used the bucket because I'd pissed myself. I was sitting in my own urine, and it didn't bother me.

"Veronica, don't try to move. I'll lift you up."

I didn't argue as he gently held me and I wrapped my arms around him. It was as if I couldn't feel a thing, I thought. I was holding him, but he lifted and held me up tighter. I closed my eyes once again and started to fall back asleep. I could feel my body jolting up and down. We were leaving the dungeon, and I didn't know where he was taking me.

"What's wrong with her?" another voice asked, but we were still moving.

"She's fucking dehydrated, gone into shock. She needs a warm bath, to get out of these soiled clothes and something good to eat. Soup or something. Tell Lourdes to make it now."

"Where are you taking her?"

I moaned, and this seemed to stop the conversation, but then it continued as I heard Diego raise his voice.

"I don't know what you were thinking, and I couldn't give a shit right now. *Llamarla ya!*"

I didn't know what the last part of his sentence meant, but somehow he magically wrapped my arm around his and I closed my eyes even tighter, with what little strength I had in me. I hated Ricardo for making me soil myself and for Diego for witnessing it. I wanted to leave, and I started to cry.

I felt him come to an abrupt stop and say, "Don't cry. It's not your fault. It's this stupid cousin of mine."

I smiled; I didn't know if I was looking directly at him, but by his comforting voice, I knew I'd found salvation somehow. As he laid me on top of a bed gently, I opened my eyes. I didn't recognize the room; it was black, and the paintings hung on the wall were dark and obscure. If I was in hell, then I sure felt like it the moment I entered the room.

"Joder! My room. My bed! What the hell, Diego?" Ricardo said as he came to the foot of the bed. I sat up to face him.

"Yeah, your fucking bed now is full of shit. She's dehydrated, she needs soup, and a warm bath. Unless you're going to strip her and put her in the bath, then I suggest you tell Lourdes to start cooking and leave me to it."

He didn't respond; instead, I watched as he walked away. I started to shake, as I had images of him pulling out a gun and shooting Diego, then me as a result of it.

Diego's voice turned gentle again as he said, "I'm going to run you a warm bath."

I tried to move my head because I was unable to speak. I felt like a helpless child. He seemed at peace about my reaction as he left me, soiled and wet on Ricardo's bed.

It didn't take long for Diego to reappear, but he didn't carry me into the bath, he gently stripped my clothes and I tried to help him, but I was too feeble. I was laying naked on Ricardo's bed, but he was the furthest thing on my mind.

"The bath is not too warm because you could completely pass out, but it's warm enough to get your circulation going. I'll first put you in the shower to get the stench off you, then in the bath. Okay?"

I nodded my head. "Do you think you can stand in the shower for a few seconds so I can run the head on your body?"

Again, I gave consent with my body language.

"Good."

He lifted me to the shower, where the water was already running, and I could see a little steam leaving it. I knew by stench he meant the shit and urine which had probably become a second skin on my body. I didn't know when I had done either, but they were there, as I could smell them. Diego didn't flinch. He didn't appear to react to my body at all.

I turned around, holding the shower doors for support, then he smiled and said, as he turned off the shower. "Let's get you into the bath."

The bathroom was so big. As I stepped on the heated tiles, I admired the life-size mirror, which hung over the bath, and the window, which was in front of it. It had marble steps to walk up to the cream bath which was more of a Jacuzzi size than a bath. I wondered if Ricardo spent his nights in the bath, admiring the grounds and feeling victorious about all the people he'd killed the same day. The idea of leaving my urine and shit on his bed gave me some sort of satisfaction. Diego was right my circulation started to work and no more did I feel so feeble, and I climbed into the bath with little assistance.

"I'll get you some lemon water and have a shower myself. I won't be long."

I knew the reason he said it, was because he had my shit on him. I sighed as I closed my eyes and held on to the side of the bath. I was feeling better already, not enough to forget what had happened the last couple of days, but well enough to be more aware of my surroundings. I had initially believed I was coming into this house to die, and up until a few minutes ago, I had thought I would be proven right.

I DIDN'T WANT to leave the bath, Diego had come with a jug of warm water and lemon and I'd finished one glass, a second, and I was on my third. I still wasn't feeling the need to pee. He told me I should shout out if I needed anything, but I wanted to be by myself and to enjoy the view.

When I heard footsteps behind me, and as I turned around to see they were Ricardo's; there he was with a tray in his hand.

"Do you want me to leave this here?"

I shook my head. "No."

Who eats in the bathroom?

Was this his way of trying to be nice? It was too late; I couldn't forget, let alone forgive what he'd done to me.

"Fine, I'll leave it on the table in the room. Don't worry, your clothes and my sheets have been removed."

"As if I would worry about that!"

I stood with all the confidence in the world, and he nearly dropped the tray as his eyes flashed on my naked flesh.

"Look at me!" I pointed to the scratches and bruises on the side of my body.

"If you wanted to kill me, then you should have done it already. I don't understand why you had to treat me this way. What did I do to you, apart from crash my car into yours by accident?"

I shook my head, wanting him to look at me, but then he turned his back to me. He ignored me and it cut like a knife, the idea he could be so cold, so unforgiving about the way he'd treated me.

"Why did you do this to me? Why would you behave this way?"

He started to move away. I wanted to follow him, but I knew if I moved with haste, then I would most likely slip on the floor and end up at the morgue.

"Your soup will be waiting for you in my room. When you're ready then you can have it. There's warm bread, too."

He opened the door he once entered, and then left. I could see him setting down the tray, and then he left. I didn't hesitate in leaving the bath. I'd been in there long enough and I was hungry, so I headed to the table after grabbing the robe Diego had left at the side of the bath. I didn't even dry myself properly, quickly sweeping my hair into a bun and then opening the door. There was an assortment of food on the table; not only soup, but chicken with rice, and bread. All that was missing was dessert and I would have had a four-course meal. I smiled at the aroma which was making me feel the need to sit down and dig in. I didn't hesitate as I picked up the cutlery, and started to devour it.

23

R icardo

MY PHONE CHIMED as I sat down to lunch; I hadn't seen Veronica since I spent last night in the guest bedroom. Diego had done a disappearing act, too. I seemed to have alienated everyone and anyone since Pa died.

NEED MORE TIME. V

THIS MEANT she didn't want Veronica as I'd planned to give her to Vendova in two days. She wanted more time; I had no choice but to make it up to her and see if I could undo the cruel treatment I'd given to Veronica.

"You sent for me," Veronica pouted as she came into the sun lounge. I enjoyed my time in this room, especially when the weather was sunny like today. It hadn't happened often lately. Winter had come early this year. Not that I was a fan of Autumn, but the grey clouds seemed to stay in the sky a lot longer than they usually did this time of year.

She was wearing the black leggings and polo which I'd left in the closet. I should have replaced them with the clothes I'd originally bought for her, but then I remembered what Diego said to me, about me going and losing my mind; sending mixed messages all the time.

"I did. I want us to have lunch together."

She shook her head. "The last time I tried to eat with you, you sent me to the dungeon. I'm not falling for the same trick again."

I deserved her hostility but I hadn't been myself over the last couple of days. I needed to expect her to be cautious and then reassure her I wouldn't do what I did two days ago.

"I didn't ask you to sit with me; I'm telling you," I growled at her. My favorite dish was about to be served and already I'd lost my appetite with her attitude.

I took a deep breath as I took another shot of Remy Martin and deliberated about trying this lunch date all over again. She took the chair opposite me, and slumped down, and then she dragged it close to the table, making a screeching noise as she did it.

How fucking childish.

I ignored it, not commenting on it but taking another swing of the Remy Martini.

Lourdes entered and then placed our first plate in front of us. It was a green salad and she didn't even make eye contact with me. Once Diego had filled her in on what I did with Veronica, she didn't criticize, but she didn't say anything to make me think she condoned what I'd done, either. At times Lourdes didn't need to say anything with her mouth. Her actions were enough to let me know she wasn't happy with me, not one little bit.

"Oh, Veronica, nice to see you up and about. If you don't want a salad, I could do soup for you again...if you need it?"

The last part of the sentence was directed at me, but with the screech of the chair and the attitude of Lourdes, I did what I knew to do best in the company of scorned women, I ignored them.

"No. I'm fine. I'm not hungry."

Lourdes left and Veronica played with her food as I started to eat. I had her warm body next to me, even if her attitude was cold, but I didn't like her childish behavior.

I finished my salad, and between Veronica's tuts and staring out of the glass window, I knew I had to work to make her even slightly sociable.

"When will I move to my old room?" she asked, which annoyed me slightly. She was in my room, the biggest and largest in the house, and she wanted to move out.

"What's wrong with my room?"

She choked. "What's right with it?"

I cleaned my mouth with my serviette, giving her my attention as I hated a question being answered with a question. She complied with my look, answering me.

"It's creepy; it's black; it has dark pictures everywhere. I have twenty days left, and I would like to go to my old room. Not the dungeon, my room."

She was feisty, I would give her that, and her boldness surprised me, even if she was being rude.

"It's not the same as you left it."

She cleared her throat. "I know. Lourdes told me."

"Oh, so now you're the best of friends."

She stood. "An act of kindness could go a long way. You should try it."

She didn't wait for me to reply. She stormed off and I chased after her because no one left the fucking table without my permission. Catching up with her, I grabbed her hand.

She screamed, "What are you gonna do? Put me in the dungeon again?"

Our eyes were locked and there was so much fire in her eyes. She was challenging me, but I wasn't going to let her get away with acting like a spoiled child.

"You're used to getting your way. You think because you walk around with a gun ..."

I didn't wait for her to finish her sentence. I flicked her head back and then went in for the kill; I kissed her, something I'd been dying to do since the first day I met her. As I covered her lips with mine, I heard a groan and I pulled her close to me.

She could feel my hardened cock against her stomach. I expected her to fight me as if I was the bad wolf and she wanted to escape from me. I felt as if she was fighting me on the inside, but on the outside her leg wrapped around mine as I pressed her closer against my arousal, no more was she groaning but her moans filling my mouth.

I pulled back for a second, making sure no one was around, I didn't want the staff to catch me, and I wanted her to know I was going to take her; there was no holding back.

I lifted her and walked back to the sun lounge and like a voracious wolf, I cleared the table. I pulled down her sweats and ripped off her shirt. I tossed it to the side as if it was trash, and she said nothing. It was as if she was disappointed in herself and wanted to hate me; yet, she was allowing me to seduce her.

I moved closer and pulled her head to the side. I noticed she liked it when I was rough, not too rough, but enough to let her know I was taking control. I rained a wet kiss down across her shoulders, and with my free hand moved her ass closer towards me.

"You liked that didn't you?"

She didn't answer, so I moved down to her nipple and then bit gently on it.

"Aww!" she screamed, but she didn't try to stop me as my hands slid around her waist. I could feel her muscles tense up. I wondered if her insides were melting by my touch.

Her nipples were so fucking hard right now.

The only sound was our breathing. The whole house was silent, no one was around, no one could hear her if she decided to scream. Then again, no one would bother us; they knew better than to interfere with my extra-curricular activities.

"Turn around," I commanded. She looked at me for a split second as if to fight me once again. She had her eyes closed and was comfortable in the position, a little too comfortable. I had to show her who was in charge.

I backed away from her, and I heard her gasp as if she was missing my touch. She slowly turned around, naked on my sun lounge table, and then I spread my fingertips across her lower back, all the way to her hipbone.

A muscle twitched in my jaw as my thumb began to move slowly sliding back and forth around her juicy ass. I waited for her to stop me, but she didn't as she grabbed a hold of the table and by the sound of her purrs, I could tell she liked it.

"What do you want me to do to you?"

She said nothing, but I heard her suck in a breath as one hand slid inside her thigh, teasing her, not going up to her sweet pussy, but near enough I could tell she was dripping wet.

"You're so fucking wet!"

I was trying so hard not to pull down my pants and fuck her. I wanted to take my time, but I was resisting the urge to go for it. It made me even more frustrated, at the idea of controlling myself. It was so damn hard. I pulled her hips roughly, lifting them on the cold table and I spread her legs even further apart.

"Arrh!" she screamed out, as my fingers slid in between her legs, and I pushed them into her.

She fucking hated me, but at the same time, she wasn't able to resist the sweet temptation coming her way, the promise of a fuck of a lifetime. I could tell by the way she tensed her muscles and refused to look my way.

She started to scream, with the promise of an orgasm coming, and made me hard even more.

I stopped moving and pulled back from her. Watching her in action had nearly made me come, but I watched, her body started to shake like a leaf caught up in the storm. She flopped onto the table as if her orgasm had taken every part of her.

I smiled, the same way I did whenever someone begged me for mercy when I was just about to pull the trigger on them. She was gasping, probably disappointed I hadn't fucked her. I didn't want to, not yet.

I would have her on her knees begging for me to take her, but it wouldn't be like this and it wouldn't be now.

"Grab my jacket and when you're done go and change. I want you dressed for dinner at eight."

And as the words escaped my mouth, I walked out of the sun lounge, leaving her on the table. I wanted to taste her pussy, suck those damn nipples, but I didn't know who was more of a mess, her for hating me and then letting me take her? Or me for holding back?

24

eronica

THE MAN WAS A FUCKING monster and I hated him, but not as much as I detested myself for my body betraying me. His touches weren't loving ones; fuck, he'd had me in the dungeon only yesterday. Yet, I was giving my body to him as if we were lovers recovering from a lovers' tiff.

The problem was when his fingertips were on my lower back, I couldn't help but show how much I wanted him, and I came. Why did I have to orgasm like that?

No, why did I have to orgasm at all?

I could have held back and resisted, but it'd been far too long since I'd had sex. My vagina was like, Hey, someone else is touching me apart from Veronica.

I had to get out of this house. The next three weeks couldn't go by fast enough. Seeing as he'd gone so far as to rip my shirt, I put on my joggers and grabbed the jacket he'd left on the back of his chair. No doubt he'd left it for my comfort. How kind of him, not. And then I ran out of there to his room, and closed the door behind me.

I was famished, but I felt feeble, too. The orgasm had nearly torn me apart and to make it even worse, I was craving food even more now.

I'd done nothing wrong, nothing to be ashamed of. He didn't appear to want to kill me—well, not yet. He'd had enough opportunity to do it, yet he'd nearly fucked me and left me in the dungeon. I didn't know what to make of him, at all.

I was tempted to shower and clean-up, but I was too hungry, and I didn't want to spend any more time than necessary in this room. It gave me the creeps. Before, I was too tired and weak to notice all the gold artifacts, which were either men holding guns, or like the big painting hung on his ceiling, what looked like Ricardo's face coming out of hell. The man had issues. You could tell a lot about a person by their friends, but even more by their personal space in their room and seeing how he loved to relish in darkness; said it all about the man.

He shouldn't have been able to make me wet. No, I should have thought about his bedroom and all the horniness would have dried up. Then again, I knew why I was attracted to him, and why he made me feel the way he did. He was the opposite of any man I'd ever known. He was dangerous, and there was nothing more exciting than a man who knew how to take control.

I put on the sneakers, the brand new Nike's bought by Ricardo, and I decided to head down the stairs and hopefully figure out where the kitchen was. I was half-way down the stairs, and realized I didn't have to figure it; a friendly face could guide me.

"If I didn't know any better, I would think you were avoiding me," I said to Diego as I picked up the pace.

"No, I only popped in to see how you were doing."

I nodded. "I'm doing a lot better now you're here."

"Oh?"

I confessed as I threw my hands up in the air, "I have no clue where the kitchen is."

He bowed down, and said, "My lady, I can help you, and even better, I can make you a mean salmon and avocado sandwich."

I laughed. "Can you now?"

He nodded, and taking his arm, we walked to the kitchen. Diego was always dressed as if he was either going to a party or had just come back from one. He had on a pair of red and gold pants and jacket; he clearly had a thing about Versace, as he made sure the label was showing one way or another with everything he wore. I loved his swag, style, and sophistication.

"So, how's he treating you?"

I avoided his stare as we arrived at the kitchen, making a mental note that at the bottom of the stairs, I had to take two lefts and not one to find it.

"Fine."

He laughed. "I can't imagine him treating you fine. As long as he's not putting you in the dungeon again, it's all good."

I didn't return his laugh, and he noticed as he apologized and then started to work his magic on my sandwich. I wasn't a big fan of salmon. I'd tried it a couple of times, but somehow watching Diego slice up the bread, avocado, and everything had me feeling like I was going to like it.

"You know about health, nursing, and cooking. What else is there I don't know about you?" I asked as I watched him do his magic.

"If you want to find out, then I suggest you set the table. Plates are up there, and glasses next to them."

I did as he ordered and even put out some serviettes on top of the plates, to make them look stylish and not make it look as if we were eating fancy sandwiches, but as he came close and started laying food on the table, I realized we weren't eating only sandwiches, we were having a green salad, too.

"How do you make something so simple, look fancy?"

He shrugged, his dark eyes lit up as he said, "Let's tuck in and I'll tell you my secret."

I sat down, and as soon as he handed the bowl over, I filled one side with the green salad, and the other side with the sandwiches. The bread was lightly toasted, and as soon as I did the honors of having my first bite, it didn't take long for the light peppers, lemon, and fresh salmon to make me want to eat some more.

"Ma always told me the way to a woman's heart was through her stomach."

I shook my head. "A way to a man's..."

He interrupted me as he repeated, "This is a light snack, something to fill you on the spur of the moment. Believe me when I say, when I invite a lady over and I start cooking for her, I don't even have to finish making the meal before she tells me she wants me badly. Now, let's put it in reverse. You're in the kitchen. Will a man ever say he wants you bad, 'cause you can cook? Of course not! He'll expect it to be your duty or even ask to come round again, you won't make him hot or even satisfied from the waist downwards if you can cook."

I was looking at him with my mouth wide open, and my stomach partially filled, thinking Diego most likely never went to college. I couldn't even put an age to him. He dressed young, but I had a feeling he was older than he appeared. He seemed wiser than anyone I'd ever met. He had summed human nature up in a few short sentences, a type of intelligence I'd never been party to, and I was appreciative to be in his company. I wondered if it was all part of the job, what his real role was with Ricardo. Was he the one who could read people and know how to put them at ease?

"You going to spend all afternoon with your mouth wide open trying to catch flies?"

I shook my head, I liked Diego. In a brotherly sort of way. Which was a lot more than I could say for Ricardo. I cast aside the fact I was eating dinner with him tonight. I wished I could pass the night away with Diego. I had no idea what Ricardo planned to do with me for the next twenty days, but I was counting it down, and I knew sooner or later it would all come to an end.

A BLACK SILKY dress was laid on the bed for me when I came out of the shower. I didn't lock the door; there didn't seem to be any point. I was sure he had a key to it or some way of getting in. Besides, I kept myself to myself and I assumed he would do the same, but a black dress which would show all my curves, including my love handles, was waiting for me with matching black heels.

I was scared.

I worried it was some kind of trick and he'd lock me in the dungeon again as a result of wearing it, but then he wouldn't have left it on his bed. I decided I would wear it to dinner. I had exactly ten minutes to get ready and down the stairs to the dining room for us to eat. I'd assumed we were eating there, or it could have been the sun lounge. Either way, I tied my hair up, didn't put any make-up on, and kept myself as simple as possible, apart from the bottle of Bulgaria perfume on the dressing table. I couldn't help but spray as much on me as possible.

I admired myself in the mirror for a split second, which was on the back of the door. I took a deep breath, then I opened the door. He probably spent a lot of time looking at it and making sure he was perfect before he left his room. As soon as I opened it, I was surprised to see Lourdes standing outside it.

"You ready?" she asked, a big smile on her face. Her hair was tied up, and she looked as if she was going to join us at dinner because she wasn't wearing her usual black uniform, but a red mini dress.

"Yes. You're coming, too?"

She shook her head. "No. I'm taking you to the dining room and then I'm going to meet my marido. He's waiting for me outside. Ricardo didn't want you to get lost."

I dipped my head. "I see."

I was relieved at seeing her, which meant he hadn't put the dress on the bed, she did it and the shoes too.

"I hope I didn't keep you waiting too long."

She laughed. "No. Don't worry. I put the dress and shoes in the room. Went to check something in your bedroom to make sure it was okay for tonight and then came to your door. I was about to knock on the door."

"So, I'm sleeping back in my room."

Her eyes darted to me, and then back to the stairs as we continued walking down it.

"Yes. You can go to your room now."

"I don't understand why I couldn't go back there earlier."

She didn't answer; she kept on walking and then I continued to follow her, waiting for a reply, but as we kept on walking and reached the end of the staircase, it was clear I wasn't going to get one.

"You'll be dining in the main dining room; it's a little bigger than the other one. Well, a lot bigger. Magdalena will be serving you both tonight."

She wanted to say more, but I felt as if something or someone had stopped her from saying what was on her mind. It was weird; I'd been in this house for over a week, yet I'd never been to this side of the house. Always to the left side from the staircase, where the library, kitchen, other dining room and sun lounge were, which led to the grounds. The right side had always been a mystery to me. Then again, I wasn't in the habit of walking around a house with a man who would probably throw me in the dungeon if he caught me.

As my mind started drifting and I robotically was following Lourdes, we came to a halt.

"You know, he's not a bad man. He has issues showing his emotions. Do as he says, and then your time here will be done. Okay?"

I wanted to say more, but I had a feeling Lourdes with Diego were my only friends in this crazy Ricardo world. So, I nodded my head, and then I realized we were facing a big wooden double-door with gold handles. She struggled with her tiny frame to open it for a split second, but as she did, it opened up to the most heavenly room I've ever seen. The house was modern, but there was something old and authentic about this room.

It had a large wooden table with gold legs, and paintings, classic paintings from Kadinsky to Picasso. I could only assume they were fake, but knowing Ricardo, they were probably real. He probably stole them or even worse, killed the owners and then claimed them as his own.

"Sit down, and have a nice night," Lourdes smiled, as she moved away from me, and edged me into the room. The carpet was cream, and my heels sank into it. This room could have been in a different house, with warm vibrant colors completely unlike the rest of the house, which was slightly cold.

I was about to say something to her, as I turned back, but then she was gone. I noticed him sitting on the other edge of the table. The table could easily dine sixteen people, I determined after a quick count of the chairs.

He stood and said, "Please, be seated."

I felt as if I was sitting at the principal's table and he'd invited me for dinner without a teacher. I was the only pupil, and I didn't know if I should be honored or if I should be worried about the invite.

I was about to take my chair, but as soon as I reached out for it, Magdalena, who'd I'd only met once in passing, did it for me. She was younger, maybe my age. Pretty and petite like Lourdes. I wondered if all Mexican women were as stunning as them because they were so beautiful they belonged on a catwalk, not serving a monster like Ricardo.

"Thank you."

She smiled, and then I sat at the other end of the table, wanting to take in more of the room, see the paintings close up and not be seated with this man.

"We'll eat a four-course meal and then afterward, we'll walk the grounds."

He was telling, not asking me if I wanted to eat, let alone walk with him, it was a statement more than a question, and I didn't say anything. After all, he was so far away from me, part of this felt silly, but it didn't stop me from feeling nervous.

I whispered okay, more to myself than to him.

I remembered one time reading in a book, or maybe it was in a movie, the characters talked about the cutlery and how it was best to start from the outside and work the way in. I took a mental note as Magdalena served the soup, and then headed to the other side of the table to give serve Ricardo.

I thanked her and then with the permission of Ricardo, I started to eat. I was famished, even after the sandwiches I'd had with Diego. It was as if being in the house had made me work up an appetite or maybe it was being around Ricardo. I was eating so much, something I only ever did out of nerves and boredom. I didn't know what to do with myself. My hobbies had long since died since I moved to the city and I was living in this big house with nothing to do. It would have been a fairy-tale to most women, but to me, it was a nightmare when the big bad wolf was in my presence.

As the empty soup bowl was replaced by steak and some fries, and then the empty plates were replaced by a dessert, something creamy and hot I didn't recognize.

We ate in silence. I had a little wine which I sipped simultaneously with water. I put both glasses on either side of my plate. The only sounds in the room were Magdalena's entering and leaving. I wondered if he had a secret button to press, so she knew when to come in. It was as if we had no sooner finished our plates then she would enter the room. I couldn't hear a sound from Ricardo, but if I looked up, away from my plate. I could see him. His eyes felt as if they were trying to see through me. Whenever I caught him staring, he didn't even flinch away. He kept on staring, which was kind of creepy.

I didn't even know why he wanted me to join him for dinner. What was the point if we weren't even speaking and so far away from each other? Fished eating the creamy dessert, I put the spoon down after eating the creamy dessert and he stood.

Magdalena swiftly came into the room, but he waved his hand as if he was about to do some kind of trick, and the only thing I could think was if he was going to do a trick, it should be one to disappear.

"Right, now time for our walk."

I stood, thinking the last thing I wanted to do was walk in these heels. He appeared by my side as if he read my mind, I looked up at him. He had my sneakers and a shawl in his hand.

I hated being up close to him, or the fact I felt as if he read my mind. "I think you would be more comfortable with these."

I agreed, but didn't bother to say thanks. Why should I? I was so full; the only thing I wanted to do was roll around in my bed with a sigh of relief that I could spend a night without waking up, looking at the ceiling, and being scared to death by what was above it.

I pushed the chair back.

"Pues, signor no habeis tomado café?" Magdalena asked him, and I had no idea what she said, but I had a feeling she didn't think we'd finished. Then again, she was right, he did say four-course meal and I only remembered eating three.

"Veronica, do you want coffee?"

I shook my head because I never knew with him if it was a trick question or if I should answer as I wished.

"Right," he said to me, then his eyes darted to Magdalena. "No, nada mas. Estamos llenos. Muchas gracias, Magdalena."

She nodded, then she moved away from us and started to clear the table. I'd finished putting on the sneakers and wrapped the shawl he had on his arm around my shoulders.

I didn't want to give him the satisfaction of believing underneath it all, he could be kind and make me grateful for even a minute. I didn't appreciate anything about this man, no matter how handsome he was, especially in his dark blue suit and matching shirt. I could see how ripped he was. No, I had to get my attraction out of the window and only concentrate on one thing, getting out of here as soon as possible.

WE WALKED IN SILENCE, as we had been over dinner. We were by the pond when Ricardo finally broke the silence. It wasn't far from the house, maybe fifteen minutes, but even then, the house was in the distance and I realized I'd done more exercise by taking a stroll outside with him than I'd done the whole time I'd been in the house. I'd been lazy becoming a person I didn't even recognize, lounging around the house doing nothing.

"When I bought this land, it was all bushes. I built this pond with Pa, with my own hands."

I noticed lights at the side of the pond, and the fish seemed to be dancing in the moonlight.

"It has fish in it."

He laughed. "Yeah, funny. I don't come out here much lately. It's a beautiful night tonight, not too cold and not hot, either. Unusual for this time of year."

Again, I agreed with him.

"I think we got off to a wrong start," he said abruptly, probably trying to get to the point of the conversation. I felt as if this was hard for him. Then it dawned on me. I bet he never expresses how he feels, and this is difficult for him.

"I'm not used to having company."

I moved away from him, not ignoring what he had to say, but he was awkward, fidgety as if he was a bear lost and couldn't find his way home. It was making me feel nervous, too.

"I brought you to this house to help me with something. I don't know how to explain it, and I'm not doing a good job of it. Let's sit and we can discuss it."

I shrugged as he pointed to the bench by the side of the pond. If he hadn't treated me the way he'd done so far, then this could be a romantic setting. As much as he wasn't being sexual or even trying to be cruel. I could have made it easier for him, but I didn't because I didn't trust him. It could be an act to make me think of him as a human being.

"Okay. The reason I said the thirty days is because you know my father was killed, and I'm trying to find the killer."

"Aren't the police doing that?"

He choked. "You've got to be kidding, I think they would dance on his grave if they had a chance. They're not looking; they're not even interested. If anything they are happy he's dead and wish I would join him, too."

"They're law and order. They abide by it," I said thinking I was sick and tired of everyone making out the police department was bad. There were a few bad ones, like with everything in life. It didn't mean none of them abided by the law. "It's like me getting on an American Airlines flight and saying, American Airlines are shit because I got on one flight and I had a crap service. One flight in comparison to thousands per day, doesn't mean they are a shit airline."

He said, "But you would consider them to be, if you got on at least ten flights and you had the same service on every single flight."

He had a point, but I didn't want to tell him he was right.

"Anyway, I don't want us to be enemies, and I don't want you to hate me for what I did to you. It was..."

"Wrong? Out of order? Harsh?"

"I apologize," he said abruptly, as he continued to explain something to me. I faced him, for the first time. I could look at him, even if he was acting like a lost boy who'd lost his one piece of chocolate in the sand and he was desperately trying to find it. I could tell Ricardo wasn't used to expressing himself. It was hard for him. A little too hard.

"Someone killed my father and I need to find out who it is. The other mafias are refusing to admit it is them, and it seems it may be a little complicated, and wasn't just a hit. Anyway, there's a woman. An Italian. She's good and has been used in situations like this one." He was talking so fast; it was as if he was excited about what he had to tell me.

"She's good, and she had two requests. One was a shit load of money, and the other was an innocent. A woman. Someone who is not part of any mafia and can do whatever she says, whenever she needs it. This is the reason I told you I needed you for thirty days. I need you to help find my father's killer."

I should have been relieved, happy he wanted me to help find a murderer. Nothing more and nothing less. But somehow, I felt disappointed, which was nuts. I shouldn't want Ricardo to want me, but even after all he'd done, I was crazy and would be lying to myself if I didn't want him to do what he had done to me on the table again.

"Right. So, I help find your dad's killer and then I'm free."

He nodded, then shook his head. "You're not my prisoner. You can go now if you like, but trust me when I say, if you stay and help, I will make it worth your while."

"How much?"

"Sorry?"

"You said you would make it worth my while. So how much are we talking because remember you put me in a dungeon, nearly leaving me for dead when I merely dressed up and cooked for you. So, how much?"

"One million."

I choked. "Really?"

"Five?"

I stood, ready to leave, Ricardo knew I was unemployed, had nowhere to stay but yet he was bargaining with me. It made no sense. I felt as if he was mocking me, so I started to leave.

"Five, then. The same I'm paying her."

I nearly choked on my own spit as he said the figure. I realized he wasn't mocking me, he meant it for real. I turned back, and stretched out my hand, ready to shake his, but he lifted his up and then grabbed my arm.

"You drive a hard bargain, Veronica Smith."

Even the way he said my name made me feeble at the knees. I would be a millionaire once I left this house. It was a comforting thought, even if he had treated me like crap and was using money to make up for it. I should have been relieved I was getting so much more than I expected out of this deal, but I felt as if something was missing, and as he escorted me back to the house, I realized what it was....him.

25

R icardo

I HATED BEING DISTURBED, especially first thing in the morning, but my phone was ringing like crazy and I knew whatever it was, wasn't going to wait. I was about to pick it up, when I heard a thumping on my door.

"Mierda!" I shouted out as both Juan and Diego appeared in my room, uninvited, Diego switching on the light without warning.

"You need to get dressed and get downstairs quickly. The gang's waiting for you!" Diego commanded, as if this was his house and he was running things. I knew something was bad, and he meant by everyone's presence, this was an intervention. It happened from time-to-time when a boss went off the rails. Everyone kicked in.

The truth be known, I wasn't sleeping, I was lying in bed

but mainly because I didn't want to get up and face the world or even worse deal with Veronica, my sweet temptation.

Before I could even respond or say anything, as quickly as Diego had entered the room, he left again.

"Sorry, jefe, it's bad." Juan followed Diego. I found myself speechless, lying in my empty bed, and the fucking painting above me now taunted me. I remembered what Veronica said about now being able to sleep better without the painting giving her nightmares. It'd never bothered me before, and Veronica had been the only woman who had ever slept in my bed. I had a suite at the Hilton; if I wanted to fuck a woman, I would take her there or my penthouse. Never my home and certainly not my bed. Diego knew this, he knew it was an invasion of my privacy. Something so dear to me, yet he'd rocked the boat the moment he brought Veronica into it, and he hadn't even fucking apologized. I had a bone to pick with him, but I would do it in time, not today.

I'd been in my room, the library, and on occasion the kitchen since having dinner with Veronica; in between I would be checking my phone. Trying to figure out if Vedova Nera wanted Veronica, but nothing. It was as if she wasn't working for me anymore, but I had to be patient, it was a virtue, I never had to practice until now.

I hadn't shaved in days, something I used to insist upon doing every morning. I'd somehow put it to the side. I put on one of my CK shirts, a white one, and some slacks. Everything I was wearing was unusual to me. I bought on the wing, if I wanted to have a meeting with a jock and needed him to feel I was one of them and not some Mexican. It could easily be done with a white shirt and slacks, they seemed to think I wasn't a foreigner, but one of them simply by how I dressed, even if I did look different.

I sighed as I put on the clothes and then headed downstairs.

I walked down to the conference hall, passing the library and hoping to bump into Veronica.

Fuck!

I could take her if I wanted to, but then it wouldn't be as much fun. I knew in time, it was exactly what she would do. I needed to be patient; that fucking word again.

I opened the conference door and the room was filled with smoke. Everyone knew I hated smoking in my house. They could do it outside, not indoors and certainly not in the conference room.

"Someone open the fucking window!" I waved, thinking someone would do it on command. I didn't care who, I didn't want to choke on the different scents of tobacco filling the room. Then again, I stopped as I realized someone wasn't smoking tobacco, they were smoking something a lot stronger.

"Primo!" Marta waved at me. "Believe me, when Juan tells you what's going down, you'll need to fucking smoke this."

"No, hola, como estas? Nada..."

Diego piped up, "We've got no time for shit. We need a plan and quick; after all, this affects all of us and you caused the fucking storm."

"Shit the fuck down Diego, I've given you a fucking finger, and you've taken a leg. Remember who's in charge. Me not fucking you!" I screamed because they'd lost sight of who was in charge, me and not them. Especially not Diego as much as he was trying to fill my shoes, the only way he could do once I was dead.

Frank, who was the voice of reason and the new member of our team.

"Que? Que pasó?" I barked as I brought the damn bottle of bourbon at the end of the conference room and bring it to the table and drink it, while recovering from my headache and hangover from last night.

"Mario está muerto!" Diego said, and this was when I

remembered Frank was in the room, and he hated it when we switched to Spanish and he couldn't keep up with the conversation.

I shook my head. "Mario's dead. Keep to English for Frank. How?"

Diego wasn't clean-shaven or even dressed up. Who would have thought he owned a plain black shirt or even matching jeans. His hair was a mess, and he had more shadow under his eyes than I did.

"Fuck, I need a damn glass," he said as he stood, and then pulled his chair directly next to me.

"Ma. She found out Mario was spying for someone and killed him."

Frank said, "So, she doesn't know it's for Ricardo?"

Jose said, "No. Mario was found spying because he wasn't good at whatever he was trying to do. Anyway, she caught him, he confronted her about his boyfriend, and then she killed him."

I asked, "How do you know all this?"

He choked. "Who do you think she called to clean up the mess?"

Jose! Of course! He was the guy everyone called if they couldn't trust their own people.

"Do you think she suspects I have something to do with it?" I asked, and then Diego suddenly dropped the glass he had in his hand, the glass shattering on the floor.

"Mierda!" I screamed out.

Juan said, "We don't know."

Diego shook his head. "What the fuck? It made no sense what you did. No sense at all. The only thing you can say is, does she know if I'm involved. What the fuck were you thinking in the first place, sending Mario to do such a job? I mean, someone like him. How did you think it was going to go down?"

I ignored his question. "You need to go clear up the fucking glass."

He shook his head, kicked some of the broken glass my way and then stormed out of the room.

"Do you think he's coming to clear it up?" I asked, waving my glass in the air.

Juan moved, and by his actions, I had a feeling he was going to do it for Diego.

"You are fucked up, cuz. I thought it was a rumor, but when was the last time you slept?" Marta asked me, as she started walking towards me. I knew she came to clean the mess.

I shook my head. "No idea."

Jose said, "Don't worry, we're going to stop Ma from finding out anything and sort it out. Right, Frank?"

Frank nodded his head on cue, and they both left the conference room. I knew what Jose and Frank would be up to, by sort it out, they meant they would deal with Ma. This was getting out of hand. I was sitting here, had used someone to kill their son, and I didn't feel a thing. I couldn't feel guilty about something I had nothing to do with; it wasn't my fucking fault Mario had been careless.

"Primo, you need to get some sleep and get back to work," Marta's dark eyes lit up as she said it; she was trying to comfort me.

"I thought Diego was exaggerating, but I can see it is true."

I choked. "What's true?"

"You are not yourself. Pa is gone, but have you even thought about the funeral?"

I shook my head. Pa was dead and I was running around causing trouble. This could make a turf war and I can't say I liked the idea of it, but until his murderer was caught, I would do whatever I needed to do, even if it meant going back to Italy.

My phone chimed and I wondered if it was Diego for a split second. I glanced at it as Marta continued to smoke her pot. It was as if she couldn't be bothered and getting high seemed to be her solution. I was getting a little high on the second-hand smoke because it was so fucking strong.

ONE MORE WEEK, be ready. V

I SIGHED. "Good; at least there's some good news today."

Marta smiled as she put her weed out in my glass. "At least someone's happy. A lot of blood will be shed tonight. I hope you rest easy."

With her parting words, she was gone. I hated the fact both Diego and Marta were trying to blame me for this mess. We were all fucking animals who belonged in a zoo; this was the way things went down, one gang would cross another and then as a result of it, a war would break out. We were criminals, not fucking saints, they needed to grow a pair, wake-up and smell the fucking roses.

26

Veronica

I DECIDED I'd had enough and would look for him. Find out where he was and ask if I could go and see Jen for the day. I hadn't spoken to her lately and I was feeling guilty about it. She'd tried to be in touch, but I'd spent most of the day eating, reading with Ricardo, and the rest of the time fantasizing about him. He knew I had no money, yet he'd given me a choice. I reflected back to dinner nearly a week ago and decided maybe there was a way to get to him. Part of me felt sorry for him. His dad was dead and maybe he was the only one he could relate to, and now he was alone trying to figure out his place in life. I didn't even know how old he was, or anything about him apart from him being part of the mafia.

I wandered around the house like Alice wandering in Wonderland, wondering where he was or what he was doing. I must admit for a mafia king, I didn't think he would be inside this much. I thought he would be out and about like he'd done the first moment I came to live here.

"Hey," I said as I found him by the pond, the one where he'd agreed to pay me five million to help find his dad's killer. I was shocked to see him tossing rocks into the pond.

"Stop!" I shouted at him. "You'll kill the fish."

He ignored me, and then I noticed there was an empty bottle of bourbon next to him on the bench.

"Ricardo, stop, you'll kill the fish!"

He slurred, "Good. I kill everything. That's all I'm good at, killing things."

He started to sob. He was clearly upset about something, but I had no idea what. I should have turned back and left him, but instead, I moved closer.

"If you're so good at killing everything, then how come you haven't killed me."

What the fuck was wrong with me?

Why the hell was I trying to make him feel better?

He didn't deserve it, not one bit.

He laughed. "You remember I was going to kill you. I put you in the dungeon because you dressed up and cooked a meal for me."

Then he shook his head as if he'd been woken from a bad dream. I left; I couldn't help him. I could tell he was happy drinking his nearly empty bottle.

"Anyway, you need to get out of here. I'll send you the money. You need to be as far away from me as possible, before it's too late." He stood and he waved the bottle to get me away from him, when he tripped and fell on the ground.

"Leave him. I'll send one of the guys to pick him up," Lourdes shouted from behind me. I didn't even realize she was here; I'd thought she'd gone home. She had a bungalow at the back of the house, not too far, but I was sure yesterday she told me she wouldn't be in the main house for a couple of days. I knew better then to ask her why. I wasn't her employer, and I just assumed she had holidays. She couldn't be here 24/7.

"He's drunk. You can go in the house."

I nodded, even though I couldn't see her. I'd heard her voice and knew she wasn't asking me to leave him but telling me. I needed to get back inside, then a man past me, no doubt to get Ricardo. I realized he had issues, real ones, and I wondered if helping him find his dad's killer would be enough to fix them.

"So, are you coming out to play or am I going to have to report you missing to the police?" Jen said as I called her on FaceTime. I was back inside, and with nothing to do, I had checked to see if she was up. I needed to see a friendly face.

"Yes, yes, I'll come and see you."

"Good, what do you fancy doing? Movie? Theatre? Grab something to eat...Hey, Veronica! Are you even listening to me?"

I nodded. "Sure, just a little distracted."

My mind was racing back to seeing him in such a state and him being nervous about asking me to stay. There was a side to him I liked, one I hadn't seen in the beginning. It didn't take away what he'd done to me, though.

"Earth-to-Veronica, are you there?" she asked, waving her hands across the screen like a mad person dying for my attention.

"Look, if you don't want to do anything with me, then fine. I'll find another friend to keep me company while Ben's on a business trip."

She got my attention. She'd be home alone, which meant we didn't need to go anywhere. Maybe I'd been in this house too long. Usually, I would be dying to go out, but tonight I wasn't in the mood. I'd leave a message with Lourdes about going out, and then I'd come back in the morning. Ricardo said I wasn't a prisoner, and I could come and go as I pleased. Let's see if he was a man of his word.

"I'm getting ready, and I'll be at your place in thirty minutes."

She choked. "I thought maybe you changed your mind and didn't want to leave your mafia hunk behind."

I wished I could tell her, it was nothing to do with him. He was far from my mafia hunk, he was a man who was paying me a ton of money to find his dad's killer and nothing else. I would tell her about the arrangement so she could stop thinking this was more than it actually was. It was a simple arrangement.

"Make sure you have enough wine and chocolate to keep us entertained."

She said, "I'll go to the store now. Don't be too long."

I smiled as I waved, and said, "Don't worry, I won't."

I jumped off the bed, feeling glad to get out of the house and to see my friend again. It'd only been three weeks since we saw each other last, but it felt like a lifetime. I couldn't wait to see her and get out of the house. I would be killing two birds with one stone, and I couldn't fucking wait.

I grabbed my things and then headed down the stairs. Lourdes was there, waiting. Did she have a sixth sense or something? She always seemed to be at the right place, whenever I felt the urge to look for her.

"I was coming to see you. Could I get a car for an evening out?"

She said, "I can see."

She was looking at my bag. I didn't know why, but she was cold and reserved, not her normally bubbly self.

"Yeah, I'm going to a friend's and I'll be back tomorrow."

She nodded. "Okay. So, you'll need a car tonight and then a ride back in the morning. I'll call Ferd to take you if you could come back for breakfast around ten, okay? I'll set up for you and Ricardo."

I agreed. "Sounds good. Thanks. How long will the car be?"

She answered, "Ferd will be outside the same time as you, I'll send him a message now."

"Okay. See you in the morning."

She replied, "Have fun."

I carried on walking to the door, Ricardo was right; I wasn't a prisoner. I could come and go as I pleased, but I needed to come back to get five million dollars. I would stick to my end of the bargain. I was a woman of my word, and tonight I intended to have fun and put Ricardo's worries behind me.

27

R icardo

I WAS SO FUCKING EMBARRASSED about what happened at the pond. Lourdes told me Veronica left last night and Ferd had taken her. She was back and getting ready to join me at breakfast. I didn't think she would come back; I wouldn't if I was her. If she knew what I was capable of, then she would stay hidden.

"Oh, you're here," I said as I entered the kitchen. I tried to hide the relief she had come back, but I was sure she saw it written all over my face.

She smiled. "I have a bad hangover and I need much TLC, aka coffee." I wondered for a split second if her reference to a hangover was a punt at me, but then I saw the way she was filling her coffee and with her sunglasses neatly covering her eyes, I realized I was being paranoid.

"Good night?"

I could do this. A light-hearted conversation could lead to

us connecting and talking like normal people. This was how it worked. I'd never needed to do it but felt the urge to do it right now.

"Yeah, girls catching up and my friend is getting married in exactly five months and one week. Not that she's counting."

I nodded. "Spring wedding. Nice."

"Yeah, she seems happy, they both do. He found me passed out on their couch this morning."

I laughed at the idea of her friend's fiancé finding Veronica on his couch. I'd seen a couple of movies, not by choice. More of a case of my cousins thinking I needed to lighten up, and we'd watched a couple of these rom-com movies together. They would always consist of the female main character having two best friends, something I never understood. Why did she always need two? And I remember there would always be a scene where they would need to get drunk over a guy or their kids and it would consist of them passing out drunk on a sofa, with someone finding them the next morning.

My drunken state led to confusion. I spent most of my time the next day trying to figure out what I'd said, and even worse, what I could have done.

"Are you going to stand there all day watching me, or are you going to join me?"

I nodded. "Sorry, my mind drifted and I started to think about something else. Do you and your girlfriend have plans today?"

She took off her glasses and struggled for a few seconds to adjust her eyesight to the light. Even with her hangover, I considered she should look a mess, like I did in the mornings. She looked sexy as hell, though, with her hair all ruffled and her eyes still glowing, even if she was trying to see through the light.

"I thought maybe I needed to be here for something."

I crossed my arms, still undecided about what I planned to do today.

"Tell me, Veronica, what do you like to do?"

She shrugged. "All I ever do is work, and since I've been here, I've done none of that."

I shook my head. "You didn't answer the question. I asked what you like to do. Not what do you need to do to survive. Working is about getting money to pay the bills, to have a roof over your head. I'm asking what you like to do for fun."

She sighed as if she was thinking about the question.

"I remember when I was little, I used to love playing backgammon with my Uncle Ted during Christmas. It used to be the only time I used to enjoy it, knowing he was around, and we would play."

"Surely, there must be something else? What about reading books, listening to music, playing a sport. The list is endless."

I realized this was going to be a long-drawn-out conversation. She wasn't coming out with anything, and I started to realize we were a lot more alike than I'd ever envisaged.

"There's so many things I enjoy doing, but I never indulge in them unless they have something to do with work. Like playing golf, or chess, or even go to the orchestra."

She pointed to me, and I nearly choked on my croissant.

"The Chicago Symphony orchestra. I've been dying to see them since I first came to the city, but there hasn't been any time."

"Time is of the essence. You have to make it. I'll take you one day. Today we're going to indulge in a game of golf. Sound like a plan?"

"I suppose," she said hesitantly as if she was worried about the plan.

"What's up?"

She asked, "What do I wear? And aren't golf clubs full of rich, arrogant people?"

I laughed. "What, like me?"

She had a point, but I didn't care, I needed to get out of the house and a game of golf felt like a good idea. We would play, and then come back and eat tonight. I was so fucking wound up; if I didn't get any release or even leave this house then I would do something I would regret. Something worse than I'd already done. Veronica was a welcome distraction; she would keep me out of trouble. I didn't even feel the need for a drink. For the first time since I'd woken up, all I wanted to do was get out and have some fun. I smiled back at her, thinking she'd come into my life at the right time for so many different reasons.

WE HAD a good time at the golf course, and even better time at the Symphony. My need to drink had subsided for a while, but as soon as I saw the bottle of Louis XIII; I couldn't help but wet my lips with a shot or two. I didn't overindulge as I usually did, but it was time for me to sleep. I was exhausted and I had a feeling Veronica was feeling the same way, too.

"I'm exhausted, even if I hardly walked and spent most of my time taking the cart," she said as she yawned outside her bedroom door. I dropped her at her room, she confessed she still got lost from time-to-time. I found it sweet, whereas she was embarrassed about her confession. It was as if she had to appear tough all the time, the same thing I had to do. I'd managed to spend the day with my phone on silent, ignoring all messages from anyone in the gang. I didn't want them to spoil the mood; everything which happened yesterday had been firmly swept under the carpet.

I leaned into her, wanting to kiss her.

"Well, you give a good game," I said as I drew closer.

Her chest was heaving, and her gaze moved to my mouth

as she bit on her bottom lip. I opened my mouth, sensing the invitation, a sort of welcome. I felt her soft tongue as I pressed forward, and I slid one hand up her jaw and up to her hair.

"You want more?"

She purred, "Yes."

I swung the door open to her room, and I couldn't resist the chemistry between us. She walked backward, and I followed her lead, slamming the door behind me.

I moved close towards her and then my hands ran down her sides before gripping the hem of her golf skirt. I felt she was teasing me on the course, most women wear pants. She wanted me to look at her legs; that had to have been the only reason she bought the set when we entered the golf store.

I dove in for a kiss, and it broke for a second as I lifted her arms and brought her shirt over her head. Then I pushed it to the floor.

My thumbs ran circles across her skin, as I moved my hands to the waist of her skirt, pulling it down and all the way to her ankles.

Everything moved in slow motion as I lifted her feet, taking her shoes and socks off one by one. Our eyes locked, but then my gaze slid over her naked, lush body was eager for my touch. There was no anger or even frustration on my part.

Usually, I fucked.

I did it as a relief, not because I craved a woman, but because I craved sex. This was different, a whole other level and I wasn't going to think about the road I was embarking on but simply enjoy it.

She had on black panties which only covered half her ass and a matching bra. Her breasts were spilling over the cups.

She came towards me and then she started to pull my polo over my head. She wanted to return the favor as she started to unravel me. I knew she wouldn't be disappointed once she got to my pants, and saw I was more than willing to enter her this time; there would be no holding back.

She undid my pants and the belt too, then she pushed them both with my boxers to the floor.

"Oh my," she purred once she saw how gifted I was, and I moved towards her, so I could get rid of my pants which were hanging around my ankles.

It was as if we were talking with our bodies and not our mouths, as my hands moved around her ribs to clasp her bra. Her breasts jumped as I set them free, throwing her bra to the floor. Her breasts pressed against me as if she was urging me on, and I kissed along her neck as her nipples turned into tiny stones.

I buried my face in her chest and then her hands ran through my hair, pulling me closer. I lifted her up and put her on the bed, sitting on top of me.

"I want to suck on them so badly," I said as I admired them in the light, then she pulled herself back as if giving me permission.

I started to suck on the right nipple as it entered my mouth, using my hand to balance her body perfectly. It tasted fucking delicious. I wanted to sink my cock into her pussy, but I didn't want this moment to end, which is why I hadn't ripped her panties off yet. I decided to keep them on, to feel my cock rubbing against her dripping panties.

I slid my hands down her sides, letting my fingers run against her waist to her underwear. A shiver went through her and I closed my eyes tightly trying to resist the urge to pull them off.

I couldn't control myself any longer, so I tugged on them.

"Oww," she screamed out because no longer was I gentle, but I had turned into a starved beast.

Grabbing her hips roughly, I lifted her and held her on the base of my cock, with the other hand and pulled her onto me.

My head slunk back as I did it, the feeling was so fucking intense. I had to hold on to her, to stop me from exploding, I was the one in control.

The murmurs and purrs escaping her mouth meant she was coming so easily, even without me moving, so I started to move her hips gently. She was on top of me, face-to-face and our bodies started to move in sync. I brought my hand down to her legs, gripping one in each hand, and wrapped them around my waist, bringing her more deeply against me by changing position.

Her head fell back, and she came closer, pulling my hair once again and guiding my mouth back to hers. As our tongues glided together, our mouths matched the motion of our hips.

I touched every inch of her body, and I trailed biting kisses along the back of her shoulders. Her moans were no longer soft purrs, which started to turn into deeper breaths as if she was ready to come, but I wasn't done yet. No, I'd only fucking started. I moved one hand down to her clit, to make sure she came hard, not only once, but over and over again.

"Shit, I'm coming..."

She trailed off and I pursued her statement. "Do you like this?"

She couldn't answer as our bodies become covered in a thin sheen of sweat, her damp hair was now swinging out of control. Her eyes were firmly closed, and her movements were becoming more and more frenzied, as she held me so fucking tight, her nails felt like little claws in the back of my head.

I muffled her screams as I thrust harder inside of her, making sure the sounds were in my mouth. Her body slumped onto me, as I held on to her, and started to take control of her every movement.

"I'm not done yet," I growled, as I started to join her, but I wanted her to come again. It couldn't be only once. I would feel cheated, I decided to put someone else's emotions in front of mine.

"Sorry, I feel so weak. It was so intense," she said as I lifted her off me.

I shook my head. "Don't apologize, it's okay."

I moved towards the bathroom, wanting to jerk off and finish what I'd started. She shook her head. "No. I want to help you."

She went on all fours and decided to hold my cock with her hand, she couldn't suck me, she couldn't take me whole. I stood my ground firmly as she cleared her cum off my cock and then started to tease my balls, not with her fingers, but with her tongue. She laved them from the start to the finish, before she started to work my cock.

I couldn't believe he was on all fours in front of me and sucking my cock as if she was born to do it; first, she licked around the tip and then further each time, taking me deeper and deeper.

I found myself holding on to the bathroom door to try and balance myself, she had made me weak, as I'd done a few seconds ago with her. There was something magical about what she was doing with her tongue. She wasn't lacing it around my cock to make me cum. No, she was enjoying herself, and the idea of her having such pleasure with it, made me want to cum even more.

"Yes," she said as she gave herself a little break and then put it in her mouth.

One hand was holding on to the door, while the other was holding the back of her head, guiding her way around my cock. She was teasing, enjoying, and pleasing me at the same time.

I felt as if I was in heaven, even if I did belong in hell. I started to jerk, no longer being able to control myself. It was as if I was completely frail at the knees as I couldn't even see the light in front of me. I lost sight of everything as I fucking exploded in her mouth. It didn't stop, it felt like it was going on and on like an automatic gun.

Finally, it came to an end, no longer was I holding on to the back of her head, but both hands were on the door as I tried to get balance. Finally, I could see clearly as she flicked her head back, she was swallowing not some, but all of my cum. It made me proud to have her satisfy me. Then she smiled as she stood . "Are you going to join me on the bed?"

I would sleep with her, but I hoped she didn't think this would be a habit. She turned to switch off the light. I was thirty-five years old and I'd never spent the night in the same bed as a woman. Never. I'd fuck and leave. Veronica was doing something to me, making me feel things I didn't think was possible and it fucking scared me.

∾

A WHOLE WEEK had passed and there was nothing from Vedova Nera. My time with Veronica was getting intense. I was spending more time with her, sleeping, eating and even cooking for her. It was as if we were on honeymoon or something, and I was losing all sense of time, and worst of all, sense of business. I decided I needed to get out of the house and at least get on with work.

There was one problem. I didn't know what the fuck that meant?

Did I go to the casinos and check out how the money laundering was doing, or the night clubs to see if there was an issue? I had Juan picking me up in a few minutes, so I was dressed and ready to go. I planned to meet Juan and Diego and find out how things were going, and to get a sense of how things were going. I'd been clean for one week. No drinking, eating normally, and feeling like my old self again. That had to fucking count for something.

. . .

VERTE MANANA, no puedo hoy. D

A TEXT FROM DIEGO, telling me he couldn't make it, and it was as if they were together because within seconds the same thing happened with Juan. He sent me the same message.

I couldn't believe this was happening, so I sent them a text.

Get the fuck here, if you want to live!

It was a Saturday night and I had nothing to do. Usually, I would go to an illegal poker game, or a nightclub to keep relations going, but now I had nothing to do.

Nothing to do at all.

I knew I had to find a way to make amends with the gang, or I wouldn't be head of anything, but more the bottom of the pile and a moving target.

"What's wrong?" Veronica asked as she entered my room. I didn't know what to say to her. There was so much going through my head. I wasn't the type to talk about my emotions, especially with someone I'd shared bodily fluids with on a regular basis lately.

"Did you hear me?" she said as she came close and then put her hand on my chest, which was all it took for my cock to start growing hard against her.

"Are you ever tired?"

I laughed. "Aren't you?"

She yanked off my tie from my collar and she tossed it on the bed. I smiled as her lips met mine and then I shook my head. I was supposed to be thinking of a way to make it up to the gang, not fucking Veronica as I'd been doing for days now. I decided to show her who was boss as I moved her back onto the wall. I put my hand in her shirt and cupped her breasts. I could feel her pebbled nipples through her bra, and I roughly pulled her breasts out of them. It was as if the bra was a thin strap, and her full breasts were always enclosed by them, dying to escape.

I reached down her skirt and was ready to take off her underwear when I noticed there was nothing.

No panties.

"You are a dirty girl," I growled, unable to resist any longer. Her eyes started to flutter as she closed them tight. I magically managed to keep her in one place and then undid my belt, pants and boxers, which dropped down my ankles. We were both naked from the waist downwards, and I wrapped her legs around my waist, digging her heels against my butt. Then my dick as if it was a radar found its way into her pussy and with one more lift, I was deep inside of her.

We were breathing and moaning into each other's mouths. I was fucking her, this wasn't a romantic scene, but a sexual one. I was taking her quickly and roughly and she was loving it.

"Don't stop," she pleaded as she held on to me tightly. I watched her face as I pinned her against the wall. The sound of her back against the wall and the thrust of my hips into hers were the only sounds echoing through the room. I was hot. I had left my shirt on, and we were both fully clothed from the waist upwards.

"Fuck!" she screamed as the frustration she'd been holding in, came out like a relief. The feeling I had whenever I craved a drink, was now at the bottom of a bottle. I was rougher than I'd ever been on other days, but she didn't shy away from it; rather, she was the complete opposite. It was as if she'd craved it even more. Neither of us caring where the staff was, or if someone could accidentally see or hear us. We were on a mission, and as my cum exploded in her wet pussy, I knew my mission was complete. She flopped on the wall, and I did all I could to hold on to her.

Once we'd regained our breaths, she said, "Right, time to call Jen."

She put her bra in place, wiped her forehead as if nothing had happened and as quick as she was in my room, she was gone again.

I decided I would go to visit Juan and Diego at home. Even if they weren't home, at least they would remember me. Even if they didn't' consider me a boss, at least they could consider me a friend or give me some kind of respect, like they'd done in the past.

28

eronica

RICARDO WENT OUT YESTERDAY, he said to look for Juan and Diego, but it seems he didn't find them. I'd planned to meet up with Jen, but when he came home and I saw him sitting in the library, I knew what he wanted to do. He wanted to get drunk, he wanted to get wasted like he had by the pond.

I managed to distract him, managed to give him something to do outside of the house, and it worked. I just didn't know if I could do it every night. Part of it felt like too much hard work.

It was as if I was putting all his needs in front of mine, buying time maybe, but it gave me a purpose, and I loved being with him. And even more, I loved him being inside of me when he wasn't drunk. He was a completely different person when he wasn't drinking, one I could imagine not only spending another thirty days with, but a lot more.

"I want to go to the Chicago Symphony again. It was magical, the night you took me. It was fantastic. You have a different side to you, one I didn't even think existed."

He laughed. "A romantic side?"

I shook my head as I flirted with him in the hallway. I wanted us to go to my room, but he was insistent on staying in his.

"A human side!"

Then we both laughed as he chased me and started to tickle me. A game we played once in a while, with a view it would end one way, with sex. But we were tired. It was as if the two weeks of constantly having sex had tired us both out. His cock was tired, and my pussy was sore. I didn't think I could sit down straight, even if I wanted to. But I didn't because we seemed to be spending more time in bed every day.

"You know one thing I could never figure out," Ricardo said as he stretched and got out of bed naked. Watching his muscles flex and tight butt was a sight any woman would dream of seeing every day. I'd seen it for the past two weeks and I still couldn't get enough of it.

"What?" I purred as I stood and started to rub his shoulders. He sighed for a second, most likely debating whether to join me in bed, before he moved away and said, "Some of us have to work."

I laughed. "Is that a hint? I don't have a job!"

"My poor baby," he said as he came towards me and wrapped his arms around my waist, teasing me and pulling me closer to him.

"I lost my job the day I bumped into you."

"Crashed into me, as I recall it. Your car nearly set the whole street on fire."

He kissed me, and I kissed him back, wanting so much more.

"Okay. Well, not everyone's rich like you or my old boss, Mr. Gold."

He laughed. "Shit, Gold as your boss, that must have been fun."

I shook my head. "Far from it..." and then I kissed him back, but he was moving away from me as he said, "What do you mean?"

I sighed, thinking I wanted his lips on mine, his cock inside of me and a conversation about pervert Gold would only make it limp.

"He said if I wanted to keep my job, I had to fuck him," I summed it for him, trying to remind him I didn't want to talk about Gold, only us. Time was running out. The thirty days was nearly up and we'd heard nothing from Vedova Nera, and I didn't know what to do with myself. I couldn't just stay here, or could I?

He pushed me away, the sensitive man who wanted to be with me went away, and a man on fire was in front of me. I could tell by the way his eyes lit up. I had to choose my next words carefully.

"Veronica, don't even think about pretending that you said something else. Tell me exactly what happened with him."

I started to quiver, concerned Gold could wind up dead, even if he did deserve it.

"I'm scared. You're scaring me," I confessed as he sat at the end of the bed, legs closed, dick no longer ready for action, but very limp, and he was waiting. "I'd..." I started to stutter.

He nodded his head. "Go on."

I closed my eyes and in one swift breath relived the moment. "I'd fucked up a couple of accounts. He called me to his ivory tower and said if I wanted to keep working there I had to keep him satisfied; I refused and he told me I would be back. I stormed out of there, all teary-eyed and then when I drove away from the building I crashed into your car."

I opened my eyes, but I was too late. Ricardo had stormed out of here after my big revelation. I called out to him and heard nothing in reply. I didn't know which way he had gone, but the house was silent.

"Veronica, are you okay?" Lourdes called out, it was then she looked up the stairs and regretted it. I remembered my nakedness and went back into his room. What had I done? Somewhere along the way I'd forgotten I was with a man who didn't slap people around; he killed them. I didn't want blood on my hands, but somehow, I felt as if I was too late. I knew exactly what he was going to do.

I SAT WAITING PATIENTLY for him to come back. I didn't even bother showering, even if I did need it. I went to my room, got changed and then tried calling him. Every single time I did, it went to voicemail. It got to the stage where not only did I call, but I left a message, too. Every message felt more desperate than the last one.

"Ricardo, please don't do anything. I won't be able to live with myself. He's a father. He doesn't...please call me back."

He was a dad, but him not deserving to be hurt, wasn't exactly true. But being killed was a whole new level. I'd been living with Ricardo, cut off from the rest of the world, and for some reason this side of him. The part I'd shut out had come to life in the flash of a conversation. I could have told him something else, anything to stop this from happening. Why didn't I think about it more? A life with Ricardo would mean always watching what I said about other people, if not, then they would end up dead, like Gold. This was my new reality and I had to face the fact my actions had consequences and none of them were pretty. They were all so fucking ugly.

"Pick up the damn phone!" I screamed as it rang once again. This time it wasn't off, so there was some hope. I tossed it as it went dead, muttering if he wasn't going to pick up the phone, I was wasting my time.

"Veronica, come!" Ricardo appeared at the door, suddenly. I hadn't even heard him climb the stairs, let alone walk in the hallway. Then again, it was his job—to be as quiet as a mouse, to come and go and he pleased. To kill or not kill as he saw fit.

"Where are we going?" I was practically running after him. Trying to keep up, but it was tough. Every stride he took meant I needed to take two, yet he was walking as if he was taking a stroll around the grounds, no pressure and admiring the view. Whereas I was speed walking as if I was participating in a marathon, and I was slowing down a bit to get my heart rate down. It was pacing out of control, and as much as I told him to slow down, he ignored me.

As soon as we got to the bottom of the stairs, and he made a switch to the right, I knew exactly where he was going. I stopped trying to keep up, as I knew he was going to the back of the house. The part Lourdes was forbidden to go to, and the part where he locked me up in a dungeon as if I was some unwanted animal. He stopped as he reached the back door.

"Are you coming or not?"

He raised his eyebrow, and I knew there was a double meaning in his sentence. If I went, maybe I could save a life. The one I'd put in jeopardy after opening my big mouth. I blamed myself, as I took a deep breath. The man I had been in bed with a few hours ago had been wiped off this hallway. He'd been replaced with his true colors. The big, bad wolf was going to do more than blow this house down. I put myself in the shoes of someone who would be in his life for good, not for the remaining two days which were left. A topic we hadn't talked about, one we seemed to have forgotten about as we laid in his bed. I was thinking so damn hard on what to say. What to do, how to salvage this situation. I had on my sneakers and I felt like running, something I'd never done out of choice, only if I was late for work or something, only then would I run. Now, it felt like a necessity, maybe if I ran out of sight, then whatever Ricardo had planned would go away.

He opened the door, and then automatically we walked in and the door slammed behind us. I closed my eyes, trying to gain some kind of confidence in the words I would say to him, knowing the consequence may not be my life, but Gold's too.

We climbed down the brick stairs, and like a maze, the lights came on with every step. The dungeon lit up, but still, I couldn't see what was in the dungeon or rather who, until eventually we got to the final step and I saw him.

Gold!

But he wasn't alone. Diego and Juan were with him.

He was tied up, naked, bruised along the side, and whimpering on the floor like an injured lamb. They'd roughed him up pretty badly, or rather Juan had done the deed. I could tell by his knuckles which were dripping in blood. Diego stood looking not at Gold, but me. I didn't tell him to hurt Gold. I told the truth, this was a life I wasn't accustomed to, but it was an eye-opener to see the consequences of words, and what Ricardo was capable of. It was one thing to think it, but another to have it in front of you, begging for forgiveness. Begging for salvation.

"Levantarle," Ricardo said, and automatically both Diego and Juan lifted Gold.

He cried, tears spilling down his cheeks. "Please stop!" And this was when I noticed, not only had he bruised his body, but his cock, too. It was as if it'd been nearly cut off and I hated to think of the screams which had occurred as a result of it.

Gold was crying, most likely because he was about to be put out of his misery and be killed. I couldn't let this go on; it was too much.

"Ricardo, I beg you to stop. You're going to kill him," I

pleaded as I sunk down to his feet. I was on my knees begging him to stop.

He didn't say a word, but it was Gold who said, "Veronica?" he whispered as he heard my voice.

"Suletarlo," Ricardo said, ignoring my cries, and moving his hand away from mine.

I turned to see Gold, who was now trying to focus, and he was looking around as if he was blind but could see a little bit.

"Mr. Precious Gold, how rich do you feel now?" Ricardo said with a smile on his face.

It was as if seeing Gold in this position gave him some sort of pleasure. I'd seen the same smile as I rode Ricardo many times. He always had the same grin, his lips curling as he received pleasure. He was doing the same thing now, getting off on Gold's pain. No more did Gold disgust me, but Ricardo did as he unveiled his true colors.

"You want to save him?"

Ricardo asked, then offered his hand to lift me from the floor. I refused it, as I wanted to get as far away from here as possible.

"If we don't take him to the hospital now, then he'll die," Diego said as he struggled to hold Gold up. "He's losing consciousness."

Ricardo gazed at me, as I moved away from him.

"Should they save him?"

I looked at Diego and said, "Take him to the hospital."

He didn't move.

"Now!"

Ricardo nodded, and I rushed back up the stairs. There were too many emotions going through my head. It started with coming down the stairs, the memory of myself being locked in the dungeon and then it came rushing back to me. Ricardo and I weren't lovers, or even had the potential of a future together. I went to my room, needing to be alone. I'd done something so wrong, I didn't know if I could sleep at night. Yet, fear took over me as I thought about leaving and the smile on Ricardo's face. If I left, if I ran away, would he smile the same way if they killed me?

Would it bring him the same pleasure as it had when I was on top of him?

29

R icardo

I COULD TELL by the way she looked at me, I disgusted her. I could tell by the way she ran up the stairs as if she was competing in the Olympics. She ran not only up the stairs, but to her room, so she hadn't left yet. I should go up there, to try and reassure her, but I would be lying to not only her but myself.

I got a fucking kick out of seeing Gold whimper. I heard from the hospital where they had spent all night trying to fix his cock back on. Fucking waste of space, as his wife would have to spend her days having to bring him back to health. I made sure she knew she'd be wasting her time. I ensured there was enough evidence of every single time he fucked someone else or even worse threatened a woman who would lose her job, even one where he offered to pay her husband's medical bills if she fucked him. She did, and Gold never paid. She lost her job, her home, and her dignity. I made sure all this landed on Mrs. Gold's doorstep. I had videos, pictures, and all the rest of it, and as a result she'd be divorcing him. But while the fuck will lose most of his money, he should have lost his life too. The more I found out about him, the more I wished I had ignored Veronica and killed him. But somehow, knowing he was going to have a very expensive divorce was a fate better than death. He would suffer, and his family would do too, for him being such a prick.

I had to swallow my pride and go see Veronica. I had a bunch of flowers, some chocolate, her favorite Ferrero Rocher, and I was in a good mood. Last night was a good result, even if she didn't feel the same way.

Lourdes told me she didn't come down to breakfast. I spent most of it with Juan cleaning up the fucking blood downstairs, and the rest of the morning paying Mrs. Gold a visit. Usually, I would get Jose to clean-up, but he was busy making sure Ma wasn't suspicious and knew nothing about my deal with Mario.

I was tired, and not in the mood for confrontation. I could have gone to my bed and caught up on some sleep, but between the number of Red Bulls I'd had and coffee, I was wide awake.

"Veronica," I barked as I knocked on her door. I waited patiently, adjusting my collar as if I was going on a date, but then I heard nothing.

I knocked again. "Veronica, look, can we talk?" I asked as I stood by the door, tapping my foot impatiently and thinking about the effort I'd gone to apologize, for what I wasn't even sure of. I knew I had to give her some kind of gesture, something to say I was sorry, or she'd never forgive me. For what? I was still puzzled, but Diego said go buy her flowers as if he was an expert in matters of the heart, and the salesgirl asked if I'd wanted to add some chocolates, so this was how I ended up with two items at the flower store and not one.

"If I don't open it," she said as she swung it open, "What are you going to do, beat it down and then hit me for not opening it?"

She had her arms crossed, dressed in the same black sweat-pants suit as she was yesterday, which meant not only had she not changed, but she hadn't showered, eaten, and definitely hadn't brushed her teeth.

I shook my head, remembering I was here to apologize, and not to criticize her current state.

"I bought you these."

She took them and threw them in the trash, then came back to the door. I was shocked by the fact she'd done it, and she came face-to-face with me, with her arms crossed again.

"Anything else?"

"Look, why don't you freshen up. Then we can talk. I think there's something you should know."

"What Gold's a dog? He probably has some babies some-where his wife doesn't know about, or he didn't donate to char-ity, or even better, he stole from a charity? So, it was okay for you to do what he did, cause he's a douchebag?"

I shook my head. "When you calm down, then we can talk."

She grabbed my hand. "No, let's talk now, Mr. Big Man. Or are you going to cut my balls off, too?"

I was confused and she was tired, probably starved and talking gibberish. We both knew she didn't have any balls.

"For a start, you don't have balls, Veronica, and second, you think if you hadn't told me what he did to you then I wouldn't have done it."

She put her hand on her chest. "Thank you for saving my honor. Thank you for stopping whatever you thought would happen if you didn't do what you did."

"Well, I helped his wife out."

She laughed. "You think she didn't know?"

"I saw her this morning, and she was shocked. She said she will divorce him and take every penny he had."

"She fucking knew, Ricardo, she played you. You went there, scared the fuck out of her, and she told you some cock and bull story. Look, no woman is stupid enough to not know nothing. She turned a blind eye to everything because it was cheaper. She's no better than he is. She loves the money more than she does her pride, so she lets him do whatever he feels like it."

I shook my head. "It isn't like that. She told me she suspected he was having an affair with his secretary. She'd confronted him about it and like all adulterers, he lied about it. She knew nothing more than him saying to Claire if she slept with him then he would cover her husband's medical bills."

"Claire? She'd been married to Bill for forever; they met in high school."

"Then Gold didn't pay, she lost her home, job and everything after sleeping with him. Linda...."

She sighed. "Yeah, I know about Linda. So, what? This makes you some kind of saint, some kind of god getting rid of all the pricks in the world? Does this make you a hero?"

"I didn't make out like I was a fucking hero. I'm letting you know the man you want to save, the one you thought was better than me—what he is capable of and what he'd been using his wealth for years to do. He manipulated, stole, and hurt not only women, but men too because he could. He had all the influence and power to do it, like all those power rats. I put him in his place, and you should be thanking me. You should be on your knees begging me to fucking take his life. Not save it."

She said nothing as she avoided my eyes and moved to sit on the edge of the bed, staring instead at the floor.

"They put the prick's cock back on, and he'll recover in hospital. Now fucking freshen up and get ready; meet me downstairs to eat. No fucking tears should be spared for the idiot. He isn't worth it.

I didn't wait for a reaction, as a memory flashed in my mind, the way she looked at me last night. Scared. The same way she looked before and after I'd put her in the dungeon. I had considered the fear had gone, but she could see what I truly was. I couldn't get away from it, but the question was, could she live with it?

30

V eronica

I CLOSED MY EYES, as I thought about what Ricardo said, and the idea of him nearly killing a man like Gold felt justified. Ricardo only killed or hurt bad guys, so that was okay? He wasn't the real monster in this story. The only violence I had been exposed to was my aunt once shouting at my uncle for being late. I was so fucking confused, not only about him, but I had been feeling so hormonal lately. I sighed as I considered how bad I was smelling. I didn't notice, or rather didn't care earlier, but after being scolded by Ricardo, I decided I was in much need of a shower. As I took off my clothes, I started to get the usual cramps I did whenever my period was due; it confirmed what I already suspected, it was due any day now. This why I was feeling emotional, and the sight of seeing a man's dick nearly beaten off was a sight I wouldn't forget in a hurry. I shook at the idea of it as I entered the shower, and the hot water started to remove not only the smell, but the fear I had of Ricardo. I'd been here for nearly a month, apart from my stint in the dungeon. If he wanted to hurt me, he could have done so; the same way he did with Gold. I was curious how he managed to get hold of him so quickly, but then again, there were certain things I didn't need to know. Sometimes, too much information was dangerous, like the type I'd given to Ricardo which nearly resulted in Gold's death.

I took the sponge and started to clean my body, no more was my mind thinking about last night. As I realized guilt had me reliving it, Ricardo's words played on my mind. He deserved it.

I shook my head at the idea of it. Ricardo had been barbaric. He could have threatened him and left it; he didn't have to do what he did. Then again, even threatening him wouldn't have been enough. Fuck, I didn't know anything about this world, and I was justifying saying Ricardo should have threatened him as if it was good enough for Gold.

I held my head back, after working every inch of my body, and closed my eyes for a second before turning off the tap and then heading out of the shower. I threw on a dress, tied my hair up, and ran downstairs as if my life depended on it.

I saw a tray in the kitchen. Ricardo must have decided I wanted to eat alone.

I didn't.

I wanted to talk to him, like he'd suggested earlier, I wanted to understand his world, and parts of the night which were fresh in my mind earlier, started to fade. I knew he would be eating in the sun lounge. I smiled, predicting what his expression would be as soon as he saw me. As I had expected, he was sitting there nibbling on his salad. He looked sad, but as soon as I walked in, he had a smile on his face.

"You came. I thought you would want to be alone."

I nodded. "I know. You want to talk, and I want to listen."

He laughed. "You didn't earlier. You made it clear when you put the flowers in the trash. You know I have a secret to confess. I've never bought any woman flowers. It was my first time."

This time, I was the one laughing as he spoke so softly, and I liked this side of him. The kind that came across as pathetic and weak, with the little things showed a soft side to him.

"Never?"

I slumped down in the chair opposite him.

"Never," he repeated, and then he reminded me why I was falling for him. Or rather why I'd already fallen for him. He had this gentle side to him, one I was sure no one in his gang got to see. It was a vulnerable side which made me want to take him in my arms and hold him.

"I'll go to the kitchen and get you something."

"Lourdes not around?"

He got up, and said, "No. Her husband's not well so I told her to take her time seeing him. Besides if truth be known, she doesn't have to spend as much time here as she's been doing lately. After all, we spend most of the time in the bedroom."

"Not tonight." I waved my finger at him. We were going to talk because I wasn't willing to sweep everything under the carpet. Not yet, no, I needed to be here with an open mind, and not like some hotshot teenager, who'd been asked to the prom by a guy she had the hots for. There was no denying Ricardo's charms; his looks and body rocked my boat. So much so even watching him stand up to throw his serviette to the side and wipe his mouth made my nipples get hard. There was no denying there was a strong chemistry between us, but I needed something more. A lot more. Trust. I worried there would come a time when it would be broken.

I had asked him to save Gold, and he had done so. If someone else crossed me, and I asked Ricardo to save them, would he be willing to do it again?

Ricardo smiled at me and put my risotto in front of me.

"I could have gotten the tray you left in the kitchen for me."

He laughed. "Yeah, but then I thought it would be nicer if we ate the same thing."

He was right; part of the reason I came in here was because I wasn't in the mood to eat fish. Steam rose from the sea bass, and even though it looked delicious, I thought, *not fish again*. I made the mistake of telling Lourdes I loved it but hardly ever had the time to prepare it, and she'd seemed to make it her life goal to serve it to me all the time lately.

It was sweet of her, but I was getting a little sick of eating the same thing. Every single fish under the sun.

"Bon appétit ." He smiled as we both sat down ready to eat.

"Bon appétit ," I said as I picked up my serviette at the side of my plate, and put it on my lap, then I started to devour my meal. I hadn't realized how famished I was until the delicate rice in the savory sauce started to melt in my mouth.

"There's fresh hot bread. Lourdes made it before she left."

I nodded, and like him, I dredged it in a little bit of olive oil and started to eat it, too. It didn't take long for me to start to fill up as Ricardo ate and the only sounds were our forks hitting the plate and our moans as the food entered our mouths.

We both laughed, as we seemed to be eating at the same rhythm, and as quick as our plates were full, they soon became empty. I picked up the last piece of the pan and used it to scoop every part of the salsa on my plate.

"There's still some in the pot, if you want more?"

I shook my head. Just a few days ago, we had been eating and feeding each other like lovers; now we sat at the same table like distinct relatives.

He folded his arms, and his eyes were dark as he asked, "So, what do you want to know?"

I shrugged. "I don't know. I suppose this part of your world didn't seem real to me. I knew who you were and what you were capable of, but it was one thing knowing it and another being a part of it."

"You know the time is up tomorrow, and you don't have to stick around. You could leave."

I didn't say anything to his observation. He was right in the thirty days was nearly up, and I was still staying here, maybe because I didn't have anywhere else to go, but then the other possibility was I didn't want to leave him because as much as I hated to admit it, I'd fallen head over heels in love with this man. There was nothing he could do to push me away, even beating a man senseless and probably leaving him for dead should have made me want to leave, but it hadn't.

He broke the silence, seeing as I had nothing to say about being able to leave the house.

"I'm not sure what happened to Vedova Nera. She has done a disappearing act. Maybe she ran off with my money."

I said, "So, you let her take your money and run. You don't want to chase her?"

He shook his head. "No. I'm tired. I've even started the arrangements for the funeral. I'm going to bury my dad and let sleeping dogs lie. I don't have the strength for anything at the moment. When you do leave, you'll leave a wealthy woman. You can do whatever you want with your life. I'll start the transfer into your account, so you will be rewarded for your time here."

Rewarded for sticking around and offering to help find the monster which killed his dad, was all he had to say. Disappointment and sadness hit me hard, the distance in his words settling like a stone.

"Right, so if you don't want anymore, then I'll clean up?"

"I'll help you."

"Sure."

He shrugged and stood to start clearing up, and I followed suit. We went to the kitchen and no more were we like the lovers who would go to the kitchen, where he'd more than once seduced me on the kitchen table. We'd reverted to the uncomfortable silence that had appeared after he'd put me in the dungeon. We had nothing to talk about. He'd felt justified in his actions, and as much as I hated to admit he'd saved other women from being victims of Gold, I couldn't forget the smile Ricardo had on his face showing how much he enjoyed inflicting pain on others.

Beneath Ricardo's exterior, underneath it all, there was a darkness, one I had to figure out if I could live with forever, or if I should walk out of the door now, before I found myself in a position where I couldn't leave him, no matter how much deep down I wanted to.

31

Ricardo

I HATED the way she looked at me, as if I was a monster. The one that I'd kept hidden from her after the time she'd spent in the dungeon. I'd shoved the real me aside, thinking that she would forget about it.

How could she?

I took a nap after we had lunch, and then I went around town to do some business. She wanted to catch up with her friend Jen, her best friend. The thing loved the most about Veronica was the fact she's hardworking; she could have lounged around the house acting as if she was the queen of the castle, but from day one, she'd involved herself in helping around the house and more than once, she'd taken recipes from Lourdes so she could cook my favorite meals.

She may not have been Mexican, but she was more than a wife to me and I'd only known her for five weeks now.

Yet, the episode with Gold had completely changed us. It was as if we were the same two strangers again and I had to figure out a way to change things, before they got even worse.

I couldn't help who I was or the fact I believed what I had done was right. She didn't have to agree with it and I sure as hell didn't need her permission.

"Jefe, you busy?" Juan asked as he hovered by the door. I didn't even know he was here. He had told me he was taking the day off to spend time with his new lady friend.

Then, I realized not only was Juan here, but Diego was, too.

I had a book open, a shot of bourbon by my side, but if someone asked me what I was reading, I couldn't tell them. It was as if the book was on my lap for decoration. I'd tried taking a nap, but after ten minutes I found myself restless and not wanting to deal with anything, so I decided the best thing to do was to come down here to try and chill.

"Primo," Diego said as he moved out of the shadow of Juan and entered the library. He was hesitant, as there was bad blood between us, starting from the moment I accused the team of stealing from me, and ending the moment he drove Gold to the hospital. One thing I admired about Diego was he always looked fresh, as if he'd had twenty-four hours sleep and was ready to go out and fight the world. He wore a black and gold jacket and had jeans in every color under the sun. He'd maintained his youth, unlike most guys in the business. They tended to start young and by the time they reached thirty, they looked twice their age. Looks were everything when it came to Diego. He was the son of a nurse and had learned so many things about health over the years. His mom was recruited to deal with facilities when the doctors couldn't be reached. She was good at her job and I was sure if she sat down and took medical exams, she would pass them with flying colors.

"Primo," I replied while putting the book at the side table and standing up. I stretched out my hand to shake his, usually as soon as he saw me, he would run into my arms and we would hug like the brother I never had. I was trying to fix things, but I was failing miserably.

He shook it, and then we stared at each other for a minute as he removed his sunglasses. His eyes were bright. No one would have guessed he'd spent nearly a week at the hospital trying to find out if Gold would live or die, then had accompanied me to visit Gold's wife. Mainly, because Juan asked him to do it.

"We need to talk," Juan said, breaking the silence.

I moved away from Diego and sat down. I knew I needed to finish my bourbon and most likely have another shot before hearing what they had to say and whatever was on their minds.

"Go on then, talk."

Diego cleared his throat, and then sat down at the edge of the sofa, which was strange, maybe out of fear.

"This whole shit's going down, it needs to stop before someone else gets hurt. Since Pa died, you've been acting all messed up. Get the funeral out of the way and get to business. First, you jet off to Sicily, which Juan didn't even understand. Fuck, we both don't. I mean what was it all about? You don't even go to the office or anything, you hide in this tower and then call us to go fuck up Gold. For what? I mean, you've been calling him a prick for years. Now, his business is your problem cause of some chick."

I flared up. "Steady on, Veronica's not some chick." I hadn't decided what she was exactly, or where we were going, but I had feelings for her, for sure. She kept me calm, at peace. This was my first drink in weeks, which was a big deal for me since Pa had died. I'd been drinking cognac as if it was water; every opportunity I had, it was in my hand and within seconds down my throat. Even Lourdes told me to slow down, which I'd been doing, not feeling the need to drink, but indulging instead in Veronica's body.

"Jefe, I went to Sicily with you, hoping you would lay this business with Pa to rest, but then you accused us of stealing and all this shit. It's as if you don't care. No one sees you anymore. Unless they come to the house, you're not involved in the business anymore, it's as if I don't recognize you."

I shook my head in my defense. "I didn't accuse you of stealing..."

Diego blurted out, "The fucking gang, have you even checked your accounts? Is there any more money missing, 'cause since that day, I haven't even heard you mention it. For all we know, you could have done a transfer and forgot about it because you were too busy being drunk or something. Everyone's ready to quit, I think Marta has because I can't reach her. Frank will follow soon; he's answering calls but not as actively as he usually is. You know he still has a thing for her."

I shot up and decided to pour myself another glass, I didn't bother asking if they wanted a shot too because I had a feeling they would be leaving soon.

"Frank needs to start thinking with his head and not his fucking dick."

Diego laughed. "Fucking rich coming from you, seeing as all you've been doing later. Walking around here like you're on some honeymoon. You told us she would be here for only thirty days—he's not listening, Juan. I told you this was a waste of time."

I couldn't believe not only was Diego giving up on me, but he was causing a rift between us, one I had a feeling couldn't be mended.

"You need to stop fucking drinking, get some sleep, and put the past behind you. We have, we've forgiven you for it, and you have to do the same."

I choked. "You've forgiven me? Tu? I don't need your forgiveness, you're the one who should be thanking me for not popping you. It's as if you don't know who's boss anymore."

Then I threw the glass at him, and he dodged it in time.

"I'm fucking out of here!" he said as he stormed out, as the glass started to scatter in the library.

"Good! Before I get my gun out!" I shouted at him, before finishing another shot and then turning my head to Juan waiting for him to say something.

Juan sighed. "Jefe, por favor get some rest and let's bury Pa and put the past behind us; you're breaking us all up. We forgive you, fuck we all had a hand in it. You don't have to keep blaming yourself for it."

"Shit Juan, I don't know what the fuck you're talking about. Since we went to Sicily, I heard from Vedova Nera twice, and she told me to get a girl. I did, and then she fucking disappeared, I can't be bothered with all this shit, it's doing my head in. I don't know what's going on."

He sighed. "Vedova Nera knows..."

"Knows what?" I shouted. "What's the big fucking secret?"

He opened his mouth, and then shut it again. Veronica was standing by the door, she was in shock, not only by the broken glass, but by Juan's reaction to everything.

"What happened here?"

Juan shook his head. "Nada. I need to get going, I'll see you later, jefe, when you're better."

"Are you sick?" Veronica asked me.

"Apparently so, I'll clean up the mess as soon as I've had another drink. You better get going. I thought you'd already gone."

"No, Jen said to meet later. I checked on you earlier, but you were in bed, so I caught up on my social media and then I heard you guys and wanted to know what's going on. Is this about Gold?"

I had to think for a second, what did she mean about Gold? Then, I remembered, and realized maybe Juan and Diego did have a point, I was forgetting things so easily, losing the will to try and amend the past and move forward. I needed to stop hurting the ones close to me or I'd end up alone.

"You better go. Otherwise, you'll be late."

She shrugged. "It's okay, Ricardo. You can tell me you want to be alone. You don't need to make up an excuse."

And she was gone. I didn't clear up the mess, I decided I should stop filling the damn glass and drink through the bottle. If Pa was here he would know what to do. I was fucking alone, I'd experienced more pain in the last few weeks then I had in my whole lifetime, and I hated it. I hated what I'd become, and I didn't know how to stop it.

eronica

I TRIED to catch-up with Juan, but he was out of the door, by the time I got there. All I saw were Diego's jeep wheels speeding away, as I watched the back of his car.

Ferd, Ricardo's other driver, was an ex-SEAL and in his mid-fifties. He was a loyal driver among other things, or so Ricardo told me. He was waiting for me outside and stood patiently as I watched Diego's car, wondering whether to tell him to follow Diego or to go and meet Jen. I decided as much as I was caught up in this whole gangster life, I was kidding myself. I didn't know how these things worked, aside from this whole loyalty thing all of them working together and acting like one big family. I was an outsider. They wouldn't tell me what was really going on. In time they would; patience was a virtue and I had to exercise it.

It felt like forever since I had sat down with Jen and we chilled, and besides when you're with one of the big men in town, getting a seat at Prime and Provisions was a lot easier than I ever imagined. It was one of the bonuses of living and being with a man like Ricardo. I didn't even know if we were together. The thirty days was up over a couple of weeks ago and I was still in the house living with him. I could leave, though, which reminded me, I needed to check my bank account seeing as it was a long drive. I decided I would have a soda and sit back and enjoy the ride.

I took my phone out of my purse, and then used my thumb to get switch it on. It lit up, and then I went into my account, and it didn't take long for me to see the figures.

"Mierda!" I screamed out. I'd been living with Ricardo for so long I had managed to pick up a lot of the cuss words. He said they were the most important words to learn in Spanish.

After seeing the number of zeros in my account, the temptation to catch a flight to Beverly Hills and go shopping hit my mind, but this would mean leaving Ricardo.

No, I was happy about the money, but it was nothing compared to being with the man himself.

My eyes darted between the view outside, and my phone. I was richer than I'd ever been in my life and I should be over the moon, but without the man who made all of it happen, I was nothing. I couldn't imagine myself without him and the reality of the situation hit me. I was in a cage, with the door open, and I'd closed it, myself. Refused to leave. Ricardo knew I was going out with Jen, he didn't even bat an eyelash about letting me out. If anything, I hated the idea of leaving him in the library. I knew once I did, he'd pass out and fall asleep on the sofa after drinking too much. Lourdes told me he was doing it all the time before I came into the house and he hadn't done it since I'd been there. But I knew after the fight with Diego and Juan, he would be doing it again. I wondered what they were arguing about?

What if it was about Gold?

But then again, with the way Juan avoided looking at me, I gathered I was the reason for the argument. I kept trying to figure out what they were arguing about the whole ride to the restaurant until we arrived and it dawned on me. The last four weeks, Ricardo hadn't left the house, the only time he did leave was for us to both go out for a walk, dinner, or do something together. He never went to the office, and he never did any business. If anything, the argument must have been about me, and the fact I was steering him away from his life before me, which was a good thing. Beating and killing people wasn't much of a life, but being with me, I had a feeling we were good together and we brought out the best in each other.

Ricardo needed a change. He needed to see his good side, and I was going to be the one to make him see his life could change for the better. I felt pretty pleased with myself as we approached Prime & Provisions. I had a good feeling about when I would go back home. The way I felt about the house, not only because it was where I was staying, but the man I loved, lived there too.

"I'll park upfront, and then you can slide out," Ferd said as we were nearly outside the door. He announced it on the loudspeaker, and I could tell all eyes were on me. Who was the mysterious woman in a limo outside Prime & Provisions? It was me. The door swung open, and I got out of the limo.

"What time should I pick you up?"

I shook my head. "I'll see how the day goes. I have no plans, and I want to give Ricardo... I meant Mr. Ruiz his space."

He winked. "You don't need to tell me."

It was then I found Jen, waiting outside for me.

"Shoot, I'm late, right?"

She nodded. "As always. But what an entrance. I like."

I smiled at her. "You look great, you've got your hair cut. And even colored. Nice."

She looked so relaxed in a turtleneck black dress and her open Camel coat. The weather was playing tricks on us lately, one minute cold and the next a bit mild.

"Me! What about you? You look as if you stepped out of Chanel no. 5 store and came here."

"Moi?" I asked giving her a little twirl of my red pants suit and fake fur grey jacket.

She laughed. "Come on, let's get inside."

There was a line, which soon disappeared as we were ushered to the top of the queue.

"Your table is ready, Veronica Smith and company." The waitress smiled, Jen winked at me, and we followed the waitress. I'd been to a couple of restaurants with Ricardo to know he was treated like this every place he went, and I wouldn't deny I loved it.

The extreme lighting of the lampshades and the sparkling lights made us feel all eyes were on us. I hoped we were in the big leather chair, the one I sat with Ricardo the last time I was here. I did hint to him about it, and as we walked on the black and white tiles, I knew we were headed in a direction as soon as the crystal chandelier hung above it, gleamed. It was by far the most comfortable, with cozy leather seats and located in the most secluded part of the restaurant.

"May I take your coats?"

I nodded and handed her mine and Jen did the same. "Thanks."

As soon as we sat down, she asked if we would like anything from the wine list. I told the waitress to wait, we'd call her in a minute. She smiled and left us to it.

"I could so get used to this. I mean Ben's family is a lot

wealthier than mine, so we've been to nice places, but this, this is a whole new level."

"Tell me about it, I still can't get used to it. I'm not used to this world at all."

"This is why the thirty days are up, and you still haven't moved out. I nearly told Ben maybe you've moved in with him for good. Do you want to send for your things, Ms. Smith?"

She said the last part with a fake British accent. I laughed, but then I bit my lip at the last suggestion. She didn't need to know what happened to Gold or the fact Ricardo had something to do with it.

"He told me I could leave at any time."

She said, "Yeah, I bet he did. Did he say this between the sheets?"

I shook my head. "No, he didn't. Look I have something to show you."

I took out my phone, tapped into my bank account and then showed her my existing balance.

She screamed once her eyes focused and she realized exactly what I was showing her.

"Oh, shut up."

I nodded. "Yep, it's for real. I mean, this means I can leave at any time."

She edged closer towards me. "But I don't think it's money or even this type of service keeping you there. I mean you've been a bit quiet lately, and there I was thinking he had locked you up in a dungeon or something?"

She laughed, but I didn't join her. She went quiet as she put her hand on mine and said, "He didn't, did he?"

I shook my head, as I lied. "Of course not. I love being with him too much and all I ever used to do was work, now I don't even think about working anymore, all I do is think about being with him. Sounds crazy, right, me being shacked up with a big-time gangster."

Jen said, "No, not if he makes you happy and vice-versa. Look at Ben and me. We're happy and it has nothing to do with his money as much as his family claims it has everything to do with his money. = It's about the man. Also, we have so much in common. Do you and Ricardo?"

"We love the same music, love arts and books. I can't remember the last time I sat down and read a book, but we both do, and as for in the bedroom."

Our heads got closer together. "No man has ever touched me or made me come the way he does, it's like he knows how to press every button and he does while setting me on fire."

She laughed. "My friend's in love."

I shook my head, then I hung it down and said, "I am, aren't I?"

She smiled. "I'm so happy for you."

She was because she didn't know everything. What kind of friend was I, to start lying to my best friend? It was as if I was painting a better picture of him, hiding the truth from her about him locking me up, about Gold and everything, and I hated it. I needed to confide in someone, and Jen had been the only someone until Ricardo.

"Now, let's eat."

"Yeah, I'm starving. Oh, I keep forgetting to ask you. Did you hear about Gold?"

I shook my head. "No, why?"

She started to talk, and I pretended to hear the news for the first time. About him being injured, about his wife divorcing him and it hit me like a ton of bricks. My life was completely changing, and I didn't know whether to be happy or sad about it, all I knew was Ricardo was changing not only my life, but my friendship with Jen, too. I knew if I even pretended I knew something, she would probably tell Ben and it would all come back to me, one way or another. I'd probably watched one too many episodes of Sopranos and this was the reason I was thinking or even acting this way. It felt like the only way to keep everyone safe was to play dumb. I was acting as if I was Ricardo's girl and officially, he hadn't told me I was. I wanted to protect the man I loved the only way I knew how with my silence.

33

Ricardo

I WAS DRUNK, tired and passed out on the sofa by the time I looked up and realized it was daytime. Fuck, how long had I been like this? I looked at my phone only to notice a whole day had passed. I couldn't believe a day had passed and I'd done nothing.

I got up and headed to my room. I hadn't done something like this in a few weeks, I'd stopped the moment I got up close and personal with Veronica. As I walked up the stairs, waited at the top.

"Buenas, como esta tu marido?"

"Bien. Señora Veronica is in the garden."

I could tell by the disappointed look on her face she'd caught me in the library one too many times. She probably thought I was up to no good, once again.

"I cleaned the glass in the library," she said as she passed me walking down the stairs. I stopped and then I continued walking, feeling embarrassed not only had she seen me in such a state, but she'd seen the results too many times, I was hoping to be better. How the fuck could she respect me, when I was struggling to respect myself? Everything was a mess, everything and I didn't know how to make it better, but I felt things were better whenever Veronica was around. It was as if she was my muse. The one who stopped me from getting into trouble. She had even managed to stop me from killing Gold.

"Hey, sleepyhead," Veronica smiled as I reached the top of the stairs. Had the stairs gotten longer or was I completely out of it?

"I thought you were in the garden?"

"I was, but then I wanted to see if you made it into bed. I didn't think you would be downstairs all this time. Is it even comfortable on the sofa?"

I ignored her question wondering who else had seen me downstairs.

Fuck!

"What do you say I take you out tonight? Somewhere special?"

She started to twist her hair, as she'd done whenever I managed to charm her in some way, something all girls craved, being spoiled and being taken care of and most of all being appreciated.

"It depends what you have in mind..." she purred as she got closer to me.

"A surprise, and I need a shower, so no matter what you're doing today, make sure you're ready at five."

She laughed. "In about an hour."

I looked at the time She was right, and not only had the whole morning passed, but most of the afternoon had done so, too.

"What should I wear?"

I smiled at her. "Don't worry about that. You could wear whatever you like and you would still be beautiful."

"Keep it coming, Mr. Ruiz and I may end up staying."

I smiled. "I hope so."

I turned to walk to my room. I would take her to the Chicago Symphony and show her the time of her life. I should have told her to dress up in something fancy, but I didn't want to spoil the surprise, not after last time.

Moments later she came back and said, "Do you mind if we stay in?"

I shook my head. I minded because I didn't want to stay indoors. Indoors meant not resisting temptation and wanting to overindulge. I had to get out.

"Can we go for a walk or something?"

"Sure."

This was the one thing I hated about women, they would say one thing and the next it had double-meaning. Yes, we could walk outside, but I didn't fucking want to. I needed to get away from these walls as much as possible. The photos of Pa on the wall, the remainder of the things I'd done were all fucking screaming in my face and I needed to get out.

"Sorry, you're right. Let's go out. We can get something to eat. Nothing fancy right?"

I nodded. "Sure."

She saw things my way; whatever she had going on, she had to bottle up and deal with it later on. My feelings were the important ones right now and they were ready to explode, and one thing for sure was she didn't want to get caught up in the explosion.

34

Veronica

I DIDN'T KNOW what to do with myself, it was one of those days when I felt nervous about everything. I was late. Not one or two days late, but nearly two weeks. I needed to get to the pharmacy to take a test. The funeral was tomorrow and I couldn't do it then, but then I felt guilty about leaving Ricardo.

He would want to know where I was going, so the best thing I could do was make up some emergency and tell him I was going to visit Jen. I was on my way to see her, but not to do whatever lie I would make-up in the meantime.

"You didn't sleep all night, you kept tossing and turning," Ricardo said as I slipped out of bed. I thought he was sleeping.

"I'm anxious about tomorrow. I've only been to one funeral in my life, my mom's. I suppose I was feeling your sadness and memories of that day flashed through my mind."

He sighed. "Sorry, you don't have to come."

I kissed him on the lips, and then stroked his face. I didn't want him to blame himself for my restless sleep. It was my stupidity for not taking the pill. I forgot not for one week, but the whole time after I came out of the dungeon.

"You sure there is nothing on your mind? You seem distant."

I shook my head. "No. Nothing. Jen is waiting for me. I need to meet up with her."

"Sure."

I crawled off the bed, but not fast enough because he grabbed my arm.

"I hope you don't feel the need to stay away from me, for any reason."

"No," I whispered as a lump got stuck in my throat. I wasn't good at lying, and I seemed to be doing it all the time. First to Jen about Gold and now to Ricardo about why I was going to Jen. Is this what life with him would be about, nothing but lies? I hated the idea of it. He smiled, but I could tell he wasn't convinced. In a way, it was good he had other things to worry about, otherwise, he would notice my other leg, the one which was hovering above the bed, was shaking like hell. I needed to get out of here, Ferd was waiting for me outside, I didn't need to bother about having a shower, as I put my clothes on, tied my hair up, and then I'd be gone.

I quickly got my jeans I'd tossed on the dresser earlier, and the same shirt, all I needed was some underwear and I would be out of here.

"You can put the light on," Ricardo said as he was stretching out. "Or even draw the curtains."

"No!" I said it a bit too loud, and I even scared myself. "It's okay. I'll get changed in the bathroom while brushing my teeth. Besides you need to rest, seeing as I kept you up some of the night, you're probably tired."

"Right," he said, and I knew for sure he was distracted.

Usually, he would tell me not to be silly, I had a feeling I hadn't kept him up. He was already up.

He grabbed the pillow next to him, my replacement and the faint light was coming in through the bathroom door, showed me he'd closed his eyes and was going to fall asleep.

I took in a deep breath and rushed to the bathroom to get ready, I had to find out what was going on. Maybe it was the stress of everything which had made me miss my period? Or even after taking the pill for so long, maybe it had messed up with my whole internal system? Or maybe I was pregnant. In about one hour, I was about to find out, either way.

I WAVED to Ferd and then pressed on the bell to Jen's apartment. The good thing was Ben was at work and Jen was home alone. If it was the bad news I was expecting it to be, then I didn't want him to be around to witness it.

I was a mess. I was crying and trying to hide my tears at the back of the limo, thinking there was no point taking the test, to be told what I already suspected. I was pregnant, and I didn't know what I would do if it was true.

"Hey," Jen said as the elevator door opened and she was waiting for me in the hallway.

"What are you doing out here?"

"I thought maybe we could go for a walk first. Ferd's gone right?"

I nodded.

"What time is he coming back?"

I shrugged.

"Wow, you're a great conversationalist. I mean why do you look so gloomy, if it is then..."

I said, "I've only known him for less than a couple of

months, and we haven't even discussed the future. I mean, I don't even know if he wants me around."

She wrapped her arms around me. "Don't be silly, if he didn't want you around then he would have killed you by now."

I pulled away from her. "Not funny. And if that's your way of cheering me up then I'm not in the mood."

She smiled as her blue eyes glistened. "Okay. The real reason I want us to go out is because once Ben left to go to work, I went to the pharmacy and bought a test. Two come in a pack. Not sure why you need two when it says they're 98% accurate. Anyway, we could go for a walk, talk, and then come back here and take it or them."

I smiled, thinking about finding the truth and wanting to put it all off for a little while longer.

"I could do with a coffee and a walk."

"Do you need the bathroom?"

"I did, but for some reason, the idea of only going to the bathroom to pee for the test has made me not want to pee. Sounds weird, but it's true. You know, as if it's had the reverse effect on me."

"Makes sense."

It didn't, but I wanted to go for a walk, maybe have a coffee and I couldn't remember the last time I had gone to Starbucks. We held each other's hand and she kissed it, and the temptation to tell her everything about Ricardo crossed my mind. I knew if she knew, she would make me take the test, go to an abortion clinic, and would insist I leave the house tomorrow. She saw the romantic side of Ricardo because it was the picture I'd painted for her. I didn't want her to think of him as anything else but a gentleman. She knew he was a mobster and far from a gentleman, I didn't want her to know, things he'd done because I knew she would think less of me.

She wouldn't say it to my face, but I would be able to see in her clear blue eyes, nothing but pity. She would think of me as the small town, Iowa girl who fell in love with the gangster because she was desperate to be loved. No more would I be considered her best friend, far from it. I would be considered a lovesick fool.

THE MOMENT of truth was about to reveal itself. We'd had coffee at Starbucks, then a glass of wine at a bistro and then back to another Starbucks. I felt as if I had to have another one after having the wine. One glass wouldn't hurt, even if I was pregnant and besides, I needed it.

I had the strength of a bull, I kept telling myself as I kept staring at the pack. I can do this.

"Do you want me to come in there with you?" Jen asked as I stood in front of her bathroom.

"In the bathroom? Nah, I'm good. I know we share a lot of things, but this is one thing we can cross off the list."

She nodded her head. "If you need me, shout. I'll be right outside."

"Here goes nothing," I said as I shut the door and walked in. This would be it, the time I'd find out if I was carrying his baby or not. I shut the door, then I slowly started to unravel the packet. I put it to the side, then I read the instructions.

"Pee on the stick, two lines pregnant, one line not. Got it," I said my hands trembled as I skimmed over all the mumble-jumble and got to the main facts I needed to do this. I decided not to bother with the second packet. They said only to use it if no lines showed on the first.

I took the stick out of the wrapper, pulled down my panties, and headed to the toilet. Then I tried to sit down and position myself so I could do it properly. It was a shame they didn't have instructions on how to pee and hold the stick, I thought as I finally positioned myself in a way I could pee and hold the stick in the right position. There was only one problem, I didn't feel the need to pee. One Frappuccino, one mocha and a glass of wine, and I didn't feel the need to pee. Oh, and not forgetting the soda I had in the limo on the way there. Either way, I'd had enough liquid inside of me to start a tidal wave, yet nothing was happening and my arm was getting tired from supporting my weight.

"How's it going on in there?" Jen asked from beyond the door, and I realized when she said she would wait outside the door, she meant it. I could hear her so clearly as if she was in the bathroom with me, my eyes glanced up to make sure she hadn't opened the door.

"I can't pee. It's not flowing."

"Run, the tap, always makes me want to pee."

I shook my head, at the idea she would want to make herself pee, why would anyone want to do that? Unless she had something to tell me, too. Okay, I would ask her later for now the focus would be on peeing, and the focus would be on finding out one way or another.

I nearly tripped as I tried to get up, even though I wasn't sitting properly on the toilet. As soon as I did, I stretched out a bit, and then like magic it started to work, I had to rush back to the toilet, in the position I was in, after running the water because it was flowing like a river. I remembered it said I shouldn't put the first part of the pee on the stick, but the mid part. How the hell do you know what is the mid part of the pee?

I decided it was time before the pee stopped flowing.

"It's happening!"

I shouted at Jen and she cheered on the other side of the door.

"Yes! Yes!"

Then, I stopped peeing, and I had this big relief, as I carefully put the stick on top of the toilet and got myself ready to meet Jen outside and we would figure out the moment of truth.

Five minutes.

It felt like the longest five minutes of my life.

"Is it?"

She pointed to the stick I had in my hand as if it was a precious jewel. I nodded and then we stood staring at it. We could have sat down, but I couldn't get over the fact it was my pee on the other side of the stick. So, we stood and waited.

"One line," she whispered. "But you need two, right?"

I nodded, thinking she was knowledgeable about the whole process and if she bought two packs for me, or if one of the packs was for herself.

"Two lines," I whispered as I looked up at her blue eyes, and it was clear she was going to cry, but I didn't have the same anxiety as she had because it had already dawned on me there would be two lines. It had the moment, my body refused to urinate and it continued before the test showed me the results which were in front of my eyes.

I was speechless, feeling stupid for being so careless.

"This is good news. It's a baby, right. I don't even know why I'm crying. Sorry. This is good, right."

Again, I nodded, and she wrapped her arms around me. I hugged her so tight because I was completely lost. What was I going to do? I was knocked up by a guy I wasn't technically with, but he'd given me a ton of money, and I was due to go to his dad's funeral tomorrow.

I'd tell Ricardo after then. Tomorrow we'd get the funeral out of the way, and after then we'd figure out what to do. Or rather I would, depending on how he would react to the chain of events. Jen was right, a baby was a good thing. If his dad wasn't the Mexican Mafia King.

35

R icardo

It was time to bury him at the back of his house, the one I hadn't stepped foot in since the moment he died. The same graveyard my mom was buried in, and the one I would be buried in when I died. I needed a bloodline, so he could be buried in the same spot.

I wasn't even sure if Juan or Diego were going to show up. I hadn't seen them in days. I knew one thing for sure; I had to apologize. I had to swallow my pride and tell them I was sorry. I just hated to do it.

Mierda!

No one had taken money out of my account. I'd done the transfer like Diego had said. No one had done anything wrong to me, and I'd gone out of my way to treat them all like shit. Yet, I couldn't swallow my pride to admit it, but I knew after today, I would be back to normal. Back to being in the business, and back to taking care of things. I had to bury the old man and get it over and done with.

I even sent invites to Frank and Marta, I wanted them to come, so we could all grieve as one. We were more than a team, we were a family and I'd treated them like shit was what family did at times. They didn't treat each other well, and I'd been guilty of doing it. I hated myself for it, but I would make it up to them. I swore on my life I would.

"You ready?" Veronica asked as she stood by the door. She'd been quiet ever since she came back this morning, she said she wanted to stay the night at Jen's, as Jen had some bad news. I could have done with her company, but I didn't want her to think she had to come back here, I wanted her to do it of her own free will.

"Are you sure nothing happened yesterday? You don't look great; so sad as if..."

She sighed. "Thanks. We are going to a funeral. I feel sad I never met your dad, and I think I ate something bad last night. I told you over breakfast."

Veronica was shit at lying, I knew she was lying to me yesterday when she left. I hoped she would tell me the truth this morning, but again she continued to lie. I didn't know what was going on, but I knew she couldn't keep it a secret.

She looked like a wife in mourning with her long black dress, veil, and black hat. No one would ever know she'd never met Pa. She had such a sad look on her face and shadows under her eyes as if she hadn't slept all night.

"Let's go."

She nodded. "People are all waiting downstairs, I think we're a little late."

I would say something to her, as I walked up to her, but she took my hand and held it so tight. The way she was acting, anyone would have thought it was her dad who'd died, and not mine.

WE ALL ARRIVED BACK at the house, the reception was underway and in true Mexican style, it was a party. The men loved it, as it was an excuse to get drunk without their wives telling them they couldn't get drunk because it was inappropriate. It was appropriate at a funeral, if anything, it was traditional.

As for the women, they served food and gossiped about everyone's husband, as was the tradition and Pa would have been proud today. No one had let him down. They'd kept up their side of the deal.

"Jefe, can we talk?" Juan asked as he appeared by my side. I was by the door leading out to the garden, watching everyone dance and have a good time.

I was about to go and look for Veronica, but I was happy Juan came, so I left with him. I could tell by the direction he was walking in he was going to the conference room.

I did spot the whole gang at the funeral and thanked them for coming. They said their condolences and I was happy to have them there, but then after the old man was laid down in the ground, the day went fuzzy for me. I didn't remember leaving the house, how I got here or if I'd even eaten today. Everything felt as if I was floating in a cloud, lying down and not observing the day, or being a part of it.

My heart skipped a beat as soon as he opened the doors and she was sitting there beside Diego. My eyes moved to Juan, who was too busy closing the door. I slowly walked in, no one said a word, both Marta and Frank who sat on the other side, holding hands a sign they were officially an item as my eyes moved back to her.

"Sentarte!" Diego commanded.

On any other day, I would have scolded and told him he couldn't tell me what to do in my own home. But today wasn't that day. I felt as if I'd been ambushed, and I hated the idea of it.

"What is she doing here?" My words were directed at Diego, my voice was shaking as if a memory in the form of a flash appeared in my mind.

"I came to put everything to rest. For you to know I know the truth and my job is done. You wasted my time Mr. Ruiz, and I didn't like it. But Diego tells me you are not well," Vedova Nera purred as she said his name. "Maybe you truly forgot all you did, and this whole thing wasn't a scam."

I choked. "Scam. You took my money to find Pa's killer, and you didn't find him. Who's the scammer?"

Vedova Nera nodded. "You are."

I couldn't believe she hadn't done her job, and she was trying to blame me. I was speechless.

"Jefe. We know you are suffering, we know you think what you did to Pa was wrong, but you need to let go. We brought Vedova Nera here to help you."

"Help? Me?"

"Prima, basta!" Marta cried. "No more. We know Pa was a monster, and it must have been hard for you. You went after him after confronting him about Ma. He confessed to you or something."

I didn't know what they were talking about, my eyes were darting between them all one-by-one as they spoke, and told me a story, one I'd kept buried in my mind.

Jose said, "We helped clean it up and make it look like some jealous lover did it, to protect you, but you need to either go to the police and confess or let someone take over the business."

I jumped up, I was in a fucking rage thinking about all the things they were saying and the memories I had about finding my dad were wiped out and replaced with ones of me killing him.

"I loved Pa."

"Sí."

Juan put his hand on my shoulder, "We know, but he went too far, over the years he started doing more shit, stuff was out of line, what you did was a good thing."

"But the shit with Gold, you got me scared, Primo. I felt as if maybe you were going down the same line as the old man. Cause this was how it starts, the odd crazy shit and then it escalates, this is what Tio Pete told me. The blood, the lies, the crimes all get to some of the great ones eventually until they cross a line and insanity starts to fold in. We don't know if you fell or hit your head. Both Juan and I found you with the old man all carved up and shit. You were lying on the floor and we told you to leave. Told you we would sort it out. We did, and the next day, Silvia his housekeeper found his body and reported his death, not you. Not like you've been telling people. I've watched you talk about finding his body and I'm like, is he for real? Is he lying? Both Juan and I were confused until we went to talk to some doctor about it. He said you could have hit your head and you've repressed the memory of what happened that day. The trauma's so bad your mind blocks it, and it creates a fake reality. This is what you've been doing. You've been living a lie for weeks, and you need to wake up from it."

I challenged him. "Or else. What are you going to do about it?"

"We've agreed if you can't move on from it, then Diego will take over," Frank said. "You don't go to the office and you've had no dealing outside of this house. Who do you think has been doing all your business? We've been telling people you're solving your dad's murder. But we all know how this shit works, there'll come a time, especially after what happened with Mario. Someone, somewhere outside of these four walls will do some digging, and you don't even want to know what will happen next. Besides, Diego's practically been running things since you've been indisposed. It just makes sense for him to run everything now."

Wow, they had it all figured out. They were trying to say I killed my Pa, and Diego should take over, and I should just naturally take a step down. He was the one who wanted to take over, and it seemed he had his lifelong wish, he was going to take over everything and there was nothing I could do to stop it. I could fucking shoot them all down, but what good would do? No one would fucking work with me again. My reputation would be completely flawed. Everyone would know I killed my Pa and my whole gang...who the fuck would want to work with a mad man. I struggled to take off my tie, ripped my jacket off and said, "Go on big man, Diego. Take over. That's what you want."

He shook his head. "I don't want it. I want you to be better, I want you to do what you need to do, to be well."

I laughed. "What, go to a therapist? Tell them I fucking killed Pa and I can't kill anyone else or run a drug, money laundering business anymore because I'm feeling guilty? You expect me to do that?"

Frank answered for him. "We expect you to step down. Just do it. It's all we ask."

Diego said nothing, as Marta started to cry. No one spoke, they were waiting on me, and all I could think about was having a drink as my hands started to shake from withdrawal symptoms. They did that sometimes if I skipped my morning shot, or afternoon one. I wanted it to end, to have a drink. I didn't give a fuck what they did, they'd decided it all without me. They weren't asking me to step down but telling me to do it.

I couldn't resist anymore, so I did what I was good at doing. I fucking left.

As I stood and swung the doors open, Veronica stood. I had

a feeling she was looking for me, I felt as if I was going to explode. Every part of me was sweating, from my head to my toes. My heart was beating out of control, as I'd seen what I did that night and it made me sick, so sick I couldn't even vomit because I hadn't eaten all day.

"Ricardo, we need to talk," she said as she grabbed my arm, and a faint smile appeared on her face as she saw me.

"Not now!" I barked and moved away from her. I needed to get as far away from this house as possible.

"No, we need to talk," she said following me out to the front. She didn't know I had no intention of going back into the house. My plan was to get in my car and get the fuck out of here.

Mierda!

I had to go to the garage, of course, all my cars were parked in there because of the funeral. I would usually have one out front, but with the guests and everything, Ferd suggested I kept them in the garage.

Veronica was still following me, I knew she would get tired eventually and give up, as I headed back into the house, and down the steps to the underground garage.

"Veronica, go back in. I'll be back later."

"When? We need to talk now. I've held it in too long."

I ignored her, even as I knew she was now ready to reveal her secret. I wasn't in a position to listen to it. I didn't say anything as I tried to figure out which car I was going to use. I pressed the button to open the garage door, took a jacket from one of the bikes hung above it.

This gave Veronica time to catch up, she was out of breath as she stood by me, and I was on the bike ready to leave.

"What is it?"

"I'm pregnant."

We both stood there as I looked at her, she rubbed her belly as if to confirm what I'd heard. I couldn't deal with this shit. If it was any other day then I would wrap her in my arms and tell her I loved her. Yet, this wasn't any ordinary day. I had buried my father, only to find out I was the reason for his death. Nothing more could be dealt with right now, and if Veronica knew she was giving birth to a baby whose father had killed his own, then she wouldn't be smiling the way she was doing right now. She would run as far away from me as possible if she knew the monster she was carrying inside of her.

I put on my helmet and left her, and there was no looking back. I didn't know if I would come back, and to make matters even worse, I didn't care.

36

eronica

HE LEFT me standing there like a jilted bride after I told him I was expecting his child. To make matters worse, I haven't seen him in three days. Three long days he disappeared, and he'd left his phone on the floor. It was as if he didn't want to be found, and I didn't know enough about Ricardo to know where he might have gone.

Jen had been texting to say she wanted to know what happened when I told Ricardo about our baby, and I lied to her again. Again. I said I hadn't told him yet.

I decided the only way to figure out what happened was to have Juan and Diego over. Ricardo could be gone for good, or maybe injured somewhere. I figured I'd call them over, have them in the living room, on the sofa and just get to the point.

"Can someone please tell me what happened to Ricardo three days ago?"

Both Juan and Diego looked at each other. They didn't say a word. I knew they were hiding something, but the question was, what was it?

"Joder! Tell me, what was so bad Ricardo missed the rest of his father's funeral and stormed out of here? What was it? I told him I'm pregnant and he didn't even blink an eye. Are you going to sit there all day looking at me like that?"

Diego asked, "You're pregnant?"

I hoped he would think I had some rights to know what was going on, they had to tell me something, as loyal as they were to Ricardo. They owed me some explanation as to what happened that night.

"You should sit down," Juan said gently, and I remembered Ricardo saying deep down underneath it all, Juan was a gentle giant. Hearing his voice now made me believe it.

I turned around to sit on the black leather sofa in the living room. I'd spent nearly all day thinking they wouldn't turn up. It was getting late and I was just about to hit the sack, as there was only so much Netflix I could get through in a day, when they finally turned up.

Diego didn't want to make eye contact. If anything, once I told him I was pregnant, he went to the door, as if he was ready to leave.

"You should get rid of it, you should..."

"Callate!" Juan shouted at Diego. He paused, his dark eyes moved to me and away, and then he moved towards the door again. He was leaving. As I'd suspected, he hadn't wanted to come in the first place.

"He's young. He doesn't understand everything, even if he thinks he does."

"I remember when I first met Diego, he was all sweet and innocent. Now, he walks around like a bear with a sore head."

Juan nodded. "That's what power does to you, and especially in this business. It changes you. You forget who you used to be, and just focus on who you need to become."

I didn't understand what Juan meant, but I had a feeling it had something to do with Ricardo. Either way, it wasn't what I called them here for tonight, not to figure out what was going on in the mafia business.

"There's no easy way to say this, but I'm learning to say things differently now. Now I have...a girlfriend."

He blushed like a teenager who'd asked a girl on his first date. It was cute, and I wondered for a split second if Ricardo considered me to be his girlfriend, or just the woman living in his house.

"Anyway, Ricardo had some sort of accident, the day his dad was killed. He forgot things, like what really happened that night, and we reminded him at the funeral."

"What do you mean, what happened? Ricardo had always said he found his dad, and some crazy person had cut out all his organs. I don't remember him saying anything about the night time," I tried to think back to every conversation we'd ever had, but I couldn't remember such a thing.

"He didn't find his dad. Silvia, the housekeeper, did. Ricardo wasn't there."

I whispered, "So, all this time, he lied to me."

Juan shook his head, "He didn't lie to you. He just didn't remember."

Then, he stood, as if he'd said more than he intended to say. I could tell he was about to leave, probably uncomfortable with the conversation we were having.

"Wait, please don't leave. I don't get it. So, if Ricardo never found his dad...he never found him in the morning...this means he must have found him alive."

"You need to be talking to Ricardo about this, not me."

He was leaving, and I needed answers. I couldn't let him

leave, so I ran after him, the same way I ran after Ricardo when he was leaving.

"Why did Diego tell me to get rid of the baby? The way he looked at me, what has all this got to do with Ricardo? I don't even know where he is, or if he's even coming back. Please, Juan, stop, tell me. What's going on?"

He sighed, as he turned back. "Ricardo killed his father. This is the problem, no one else did it. He did it all, and Diego and I cleared up the mess."

I repeated, "He killed his own father."

"Yes."

Juan moved in the direction he was moving and left. The same way Ricardo had done, but I felt too frail to follow this time. I had money. I didn't need to stay here. But the shock of it all was too much to handle and I dropped to the ground. There was no one to save me from this madness, and I realized why Diego had said what he did. As crazy as it sounded at the time, now it made perfect sense.

What kind of monster was Ricardo, to have killed his father?

37

R icardo

IT'D BEEN a week since I left home. I knew I shouldn't have left Veronica. I should have told her something, anything, including letting her know it had nothing to do with finding out about the baby. I had so much shit making me feel as if I was going crazy running through my mind. I'd suppressed the memory of killing Pa, and I needed to get it all out. I needed to relive the nightmare of the night, to know step-by-step what happened, and to know I was the one who was capable of committing it. I'd suppressed my memory so much so, I'd gone on a wild goose chase. I'd let Juan think I'd gone completely insane, by trying to find Pa's killer, when all along it was me.

Veronica was in the library when I came home, all curled up on a chair reading, and I didn't hesitate in telling her what was going on in my head. I knew there was no way I could ever forgive myself, but I had to know if she could do it, or rather if she would?

"I'm a fucking monster," I repeated, over and over again.

Veronica didn't say anything as she heard my confession. I fell to my knees as if I was in church and she was my priestess, ready to give me my penance for renouncing my sins.

"Diego and Juan told me everything. Then again, maybe not everything, but the important part and why you stormed out of your father's funeral. I don't get it. Why go to Sicily?"

I said as my throat tightened, "I don't know..."

She hesitated as she opened and closed her mouth. I was sobbing, as I tried to ask for mercy, but I retold the tale. The one I hadn't been able to tell from the beginning, but as she said, if I wanted her in my life, if I wanted her to stay, I had to tell her everything because if she one day found out I was lying, she would be gone.

"I'd turned a blind eye to dad's unhealthy obsession with women, and girls, little children pretending it didn't matter. We killed, we were all monsters. It was no different from me killing a man, to what he did."

"But he did more than that, you killed people in the business, he killed women, kids because they were poor, and they turned to him to survive and he abused it."

I nodded in agreement. This was what I had told her, and it was the truth.

"What I can't understand is, if you'd turned a blind eye to it... not only the abuse you suffered at his hand, but the abuse he inflicted on others, why did it drive you mad? Why did you feel the need to take matters into your own hand?"

I sighed, as I got up from my knees. Telling the truth was hard, so much harder than I'd ever imagined.

"Because I found out what he did to Ma. The truth, not the bullshit story, he told me. I found out she wanted us to run away, she wanted me out of this life, and I'd stayed, he made me stay. He fucking made me kill some people claiming they were part of the circuit who killed Ma. All one fucking big lie."

She took my hand. "How did you find out?"

"My Uncle Pete left me a letter as part of his will. Funny, at the time I dismissed it, I remember not even telling Pa about it. Then, one thing led to the next and I read the letter. I read every sordid thing he did to her, he punished her like a dog. He had a dungeon like the one you stayed in."

I looked away, ashamed of my actions in the past, knowing I couldn't ask anything of her. I didn't fucking deserve it. "But he let his crew rape her one by one. He shaved her. Fuck, you don't want to know."

I didn't wait for a response, as I continued to tell the horrid past and fate of my mother. The one person who truly loved me and never did me any harm.

"Did you regret it?"

"What?" I asked as if I'd been woken up from a nightmare. I was talking and forgetting I was confessing because it was the first time I'd felt any sense of relief.

"I expected killing him to make me feel better, I would feel human again, not a monster. I wouldn't let him harm others and especially me. I had a sense of relief, knowing I wouldn't come home one day, and he would hold a gun to my head, make me get down on one knee and beg for mercy. Or he wouldn't be raping any little girls. I felt free of his torture not only of me, but of others too. Knowing he was gone made me feel better. I never believed in therapy, or even talking about things bothering me. Yet, talking to you has helped. A lot."

She smiled. "It should because the idea you tried to help proves the one thing you've been saying all along: you're not a monster. You're nothing like him."

I nearly choked on my words as I said, "If you knew all the things I've done, then you wouldn't say..."

"True. I know you're not a saint, but I do know you have

saved women and children from the hand of your Pa. The women you have saved, by killing your dad, shows you have a heart. Whereas he had none."

She was smiling at me, holding my hand and trying to console me, but it didn't take away the one thing I was feeling right now, which was anxiety. I needed to know if she was going to stay with me.

"I need time, Ricardo. This has all been a little too much."

I nodded. "I know."

Then, I kissed her on the cheek and left her alone in the library, the one place I always felt solace. I had no idea what I was going to do now. It would be only a matter of time before word got out and everyone knew what I'd done. I'd have to get out of the business. My life, culture, the thing I'd known all my life, in the one way I'd never expected...I'd dug my own grave. I had a child who would be brought into this world who I had no intention of letting him go down the same road. I needed to change my life. I didn't have a clue how I was going to do it, but I knew with Veronica by my side, I would find it.

38

eronica

IT'D BEEN FOUR MONTHS, two weeks and five days since I had last seen Ricardo. Luckily, with Jen's wedding on the way, I didn't have the time to think about the next steps. His house was on the market, his penthouse, and pretty much all his goods, with from the sale going to charity. The house was bought by some rich merchant bankers; the penthouse was taking a little while to shift. I must admit, it was taking a lot longer than I'd expected. I did keep an eye on it.

Then, again I kept an eye on a lot of things ever since the day he left me in the library.

Why didn't he chase after me?

"If you're going to come and be part of my wedding with a long face, then you might as well go home. I don't want miserable people at my wedding," Jen said as she lifted her glass and had obviously drunk a little bit too much champagne.

"I need to get you down the aisle or Ben will kill me."

She laughed. "I'll kill you if you don't smile."

Maybe I'd spent too much time, with Ricardo, but whenever someone mentioned the word kill, it sent a shiver down my spine. She could probably tell all the blood had rushed out of my face as she said it, then she hugged me. We didn't need to speak. I was missing Ricardo. There was no doubt about it, and as much as I wanted him here, another part of me was glad he was as far away from us as possible. Maybe he was dead, maybe someone told someone who had found out he'd broken this so-called code and they went after him. Who knew? Only them and Ricardo. I couldn't put our unborn child's life in jeopardy; my job as a mother would be over before it'd even began, no this was for the best. In time, I would forget about him, in time I'd be able to move on properly. All I needed was time.

"We are late, so late," I screamed as I looked at the analog clock which hung on the wall and realized we should be down in reception and I should be getting her down aisle.

She shook her head. "We can't go yet."

"Yes, we can."

As I moved her arms away from mine, I noticed she hung on to me for support and not as a show of affection. She'd had a little more than one extra glass of champagne. As my gaze darted to where she'd been sitting a few seconds ago, there were three empty flutes on the table.

"Jen, please tell me you didn't drink all of them?"

She pouted, as she nodded. Her mom quickly came to the rescue as she said, "You've got bride jitters, nothing new. Drink all of it. It'll sober you up."

The coffee was so strong, even the little man inside of me, did a little cartwheel as I smelled it and moved away from them both. Coffee was a strange scent to me at the moment, it did one of two things, either made me very alert or want to be sick. I was relieved my sickness had died down, my doctor told me it would stop after the first trimester but I was well into my second trimester and I was still on occasion being sick. I still had yet to figure out why they called it morning sickness, when that was the only time of day I wasn't sick.

Across the room sat the other bridesmaids, and they were detached from us, they were Ben's side of the family, his sisters and soon to be Jen's sister-in-law. It was clear from day one they didn't like Jen; they believed she was some gold digger. Sure, Jen's family wasn't rich like them, but they were proud and Jen's dad wouldn't hear of it as his family tried to dominate the wedding and claim to want to help out financially. As a gesture of goodwill Jen allowed his sisters to be bridesmaids, even though it was clear there was bad blood between them.

"Is she ok?" One of them blurted while straightening her dress. She admired herself in the mirror, the same thing she did when she saw Jen in her dress. What bridesmaid was more worried about their appearance on the wedding day than the bride's?

The dreadful twins Ivy and Poison, which was our Jen and my nickname for them, but they were called Brooke and Belle. His parents had a thing about the B's a tradition in their family, a strange one. Each family had a letter and they would go down the alphabet to name their child. The real reason why Jen was nervous and had one too many champagne glasses was about joining Ben's family and becoming one of them.

"She's fine," I shouted back. Brooke didn't seem to care, as she finished admiring her pink silk bridesmaid dress and walked back to her sister, who sat by the window looking out of it. She was probably watching people smoke on the grounds, wishing she was one of them.

"Right, are you feeling better Jen?" I asked as I walked up to her and then I began to stroke her hair. She said her Grandma would do it to her as a kid, she would stroke her hair whenever she was nervous, and it seemed to give her comfort. Her sky blue eyes looked up at me with tears in her eyes, and I knew she was alright and we were ready to get this show on the road.

"Ready?" I smiled and she nodded as confirmation and then she put the remains of the coffee which would bring anyone back to life down on the table.

Her mom was trying to get the girls engaged and interested in the wedding, she was wasting her time. The only reason they were here, was because they wanted to find themselves a date, or maybe a boyfriend. I didn't know which one it was because they were only twenty-one, but their attitude and concept of life made me forget they were in their twenties and made me always think of them as a couple of girls in their teens.

Brooklyn said, "About time. We're late. I know the bride is supposed to be late, but this is ridiculous."

Then, they huffed.

I hated to admit she was right, I was thinking we were only a few minutes late, I didn't realize it was nearly thirty minutes.

"Here's to being the next Mrs. Cromsone."

I was so proud of her. She was putting love first. As much as she hated Ben's family, she knew their lives together would be special. I hated the idea maybe I was making a mistake. Maybe I should have taken a chance with Ricardo too and left with him. If things had gone bad I could have run away like his mom did, but what his dad did to his mom was the reason I stayed away and decided we had to end things.

I could end up like his mom.

Maybe being a monster did run in his family, and sooner rather than later Ricardo would end up like his dad.

Then again, maybe it didn't, and I should have given him another chance.

~

I WAS THE CHIEF BRIDESMAID, but I knew hardly anyone at the wedding apart from the groom and a couple of his friends, the best man, and Jen's parents. The rest were strangers. Even her friends I'd been out with on occasion were strangers to me.

Ben's mom sighed as I stood watching Jen and Ben take their first dance. I was standing in a corner, trying to stretch my legs a bit. Sitting for too long, just made my ankles swell, and standing too long, didn't make me feel much better.

"You could have made sure the bride was on time, or a little late. Forty minutes, it must be because of your condition," Ben's mom said to me with disappointment in her eyes.

"Condition?" I questioned.

She nodded. "Unmarried, pregnant, and soon-to-be single mom. Imagine the photos."

Brooke appeared on my other side and said, "Don't worry, mommy. I tried to make sure she wasn't in many."

It dawned on me why the photographer would shout the names, and then why he kept changing them. They'd masterminded a plan to keep me out of the wedding as much as possible. Until now, I hadn't realized they hated the idea of me being the chief bridesmaid because I was pregnant. Jen had managed to hide it from me.

"I should have been chief like we all wanted. But Jen didn't agree. Now, she's one of us, I'm sure she'll understand our way of thinking," Brooke said proudly, and then I started to move away from them. I couldn't stand listening to any more of this.

I held back the tears, as I decided I would wish my best friend well as she embarked on her journey as a new wife. She'd taken a quick drink break and I managed to grab her, as like Ricardo after I wished her goodbye, I'd disappear. I would be alone, with the comfort and knowledge of being a good mom to my child.

I pulled away from her embrace, saying, "Go join them on the dance floor, I'm going to fix my face."

She nodded. "Make sure you come and dance with me. You did a fantastic job today."

I smiled at her as I walked away and she went on the dance floor to join the wedding party.

"Good luck, my best friend," I sobbed as I walked away, not having a clue where I was going, or even caring about it. I knew I had to leave Chicago, and I had to do it tonight.

39

R icardo

OUR BABY WAS due any day now. I shouldn't have thought about him, but I couldn't help myself. I couldn't help but wonder if he would have his mom's dark eyes or my hazel eyes. If he would grow up knowing the man I used to be, or if he would grow up thinking I was some jock who had abandoned him and his mom when she was pregnant. Somehow the idea of my son thinking I was some jock gave me some comfort, knowing Veronica would protect my honor and his too. She wouldn't let him know he was a part of the Ruiz family. I liked it that way, and I was sure Veronica would too.

I'd only known her for weeks, but the time we'd spent together felt like a lifetime. The best time of my life, making me a better man. I smiled at the idea of it, as I shoveled the snow. The road was blocked and I'd had about three emergency calls to get the road unblocked as soon as possible. Winter had come early this year. There were blocked roads and my former boss left Alaska to go to sunnier skies, Mexico of all places. He asked if I'd been there before. I lied, telling him I couldn't even speak Spanish. I did whenever someone asked me, every part of me died the moment I left Chicago and I didn't want any of it to come back. My life here was good, humble, my dad would probably laugh from beyond his grave at the type of life I'd settled for, but it was what I'd wanted, what I needed to do. I needed to work for a living, understand the meaning of not being able to pay my rent if I didn't earn enough in a month.

Since, leaving Chicago, I'd been a cleaner, bartender, and somehow along the line, someone was talking about life in Alaska. With a flip of a coin, a map in front of me, I ended up here in Nome. Questions were asked about where I was from, but no one asked why I ended up here. My old boss, before he retired, told me people only came here to get away from whatever demon was chasing them from wherever they came from. He was right. It was by pure luck I met him in a bar and asked what he did for a living. He told me he was retiring and I could take over the business. He taught me how to fix an engine and left me for warmer temperatures. He'd lived in Nome all his life and the idea of leaving was hopeful for him. One he wouldn't die in the snow, like his father and his father before him.

I gave him a little something, more of a big something via Juan. I asked him not only to enjoy his time in Mexico but managed to send him the money I put to the side in case my son needed it in the future. I refused to touch a penny of it. I refused to live the privileged life I'd had so many years before. This was my life now, and I wouldn't give it up for anything. Well, I would for someone if she wanted to know where I was and wanted to give us a chance.

She made it clear, though, it wasn't an option. I'd waited for her in the house. In my room, the time I left her in the library. I waited a whole week. I needed her to come to me, and not the other way around; I'd given her a gift, to make public if she wished and she took it.

She published the life Pa had lived by handing it to a reporter who handed in his job and published a book. Everything was in the book, even the children and women he'd killed and some of those people wanted my life in replacement for the damage to their family. I didn't blame them, there would have been a time I would have done the same, but that time was well and truly past.

I kept in touch with Juan once in a while; he was with his wife and child in Sicily. Our conversations would start with him asking how I was and if I was keeping well and end a few seconds later with him telling me he was good and so was his wife and daughter. Never in a million years, would I have believed a trip to Sicily to hire Vedova Nera would end up with Juan falling in love again. Something he vowed could never happen. The saying, never say never was right, especially in his case. I was happy for him. He sent me a photo or two whenever I called him on a burner phone. I only called him once every two months, to let him know I was still alive, and I spoke to him, to make sure he was, too.

We didn't talk about anyone else, especially Diego. The man I handed it all to. He'd turned from a compassionate man to one who wanted to rule. I let him. Someone had to, and I was sure he was doing what he needed to do. Or felt he needed to do, the same way I did.

"Lucas!" My new name was called out by my landlady. I rented a small cabin at the end of the street. It was cheap and had everything I needed. A small bed, fridge and a stove was my life now, simple and I loved it.

"Hi, Monica. How are you today?"

She smiled. "Good. Something came for you today."

My body froze as she said the words, the idea of someone knowing exactly where I was, meant tonight, even with my new identity, I would have to be on the run. I would have to find somewhere else to live.

She rubbed her hands together.

I came to her cabin to give her rent money, but luckily if I hadn't made a stop, I wouldn't have known to make a run for it.

"She's waiting inside your cabin."

I shook my head. "Sorry. I thought you said something came for me today."

She choked. "I couldn't help it. I'm old-fashioned, and besides, you look lonely. I have a feeling she's the reason for it. They both are."

Then she winked at me, I did have to make a run, but not in the direction I was thinking of. Had Veronica come all this way?

How did she find me?

And she brought our baby with her.

Curiosity got the better of me, as I stuffed the envelope in Monica's hand and jumped in my truck so fucking fast in the snow to get home and see if my ears were deceiving me. Was I to meet my son and hopefully, my future wife, if she would have me?

40

eronica

I DIDN'T KNOW if this was a good idea, I'd only given birth over a month ago and here I was traveling with a newborn and coming to see the one man I had planned to stay away from as far as possible. He was a monster, I kept telling myself, but then it was clear I was kidding myself.

I loved him.

Even more when I saw our son's hazel eyes and knew he was a replica of his father. The man I loved and pushed away. I had to, not only for his sanity, but mine too.

I heard the engine outside and I knew it was him, the man I'd been trying to avoid, but couldn't stay away from.

I held our baby close to me, as the door swung open. His landlady said he'd been here for four months. She wanted us to wait in her cabin, but I told her Lucas wouldn't mind us waiting in his, she assumed it was a surprise and smiled as I told her the assumption was correct.

Maybe this was a mistake. The car pull up outside, but Ricardo hadn't entered the cabin. Maybe, he'd run, scared about coming inside. I looked at the baby boy, who was fast asleep on his bed, I'd put a blanket on top of him and I decided to be brave and open the door. Before I did, I grabbed my jacket. Even the winters in Chicago couldn't prepare me for the temperatures here. As I opened the door, Ricardo was on the other side, frozen as if in time.

"It's true," he whispered as he looked at me. I couldn't see much of his face, the cold wind was blowing and the ice, had me shivering, so I edged him to come inside.

"Come in, please. It's cold."

He nodded, and then he followed me inside. It was funny, seeing him as he slowly stripped off his jacket to reveal a jersey polo and jeans. The Ricardo I knew always had fancy suits, cars, and always was clean-shaven; the man in front of me was nothing like the man I knew. If anything, he was more down-to-earth, someone I would see back home who probably worked as the local mechanic. He had a beard, well-shaped, and a mustache too. His hair was cut short, but those eyes, there was no escaping them even under all that hair. We stood admiring each other, familiarizing each other with our appearances, then Rik made a sound and he smiled as his gaze darted towards him.

"It's him?"

I nodded and waited for him to ask if he could pick him up or something, but he said nothing as he got a little closer. The man I knew would have stormed into the room, made some sexual gesture and then taken Rik with no hesitation. The man in front of me was a complete stranger. I wondered if I'd made a mistake coming because he stood at the end of the bed smiling at him, too afraid to go any closer.

No more was Ricardo Ruiz a monster, he was more like a gentle giant. I should have been happy about the change, felt safe about it. I reminded myself about why I did come here, and as he stood there, I realized I'd done the right thing not staying away. I wanted him to be part of our son's life.

41

R icardo

I DIDN'T KNOW how long she'd driven or if she was still lived in Chicago. I should have asked her something. Anything, but I couldn't take my eyes of this beautiful creature in front of me, our son.

He was so innocent, and as I drew closer, I could smell him. The smell of a newborn was supposed to be a touch of heaven. I hated the idea of admitting that until now, I hadn't been near a newborn child. No one had ever asked if I wanted to hold one, and quite frankly until now I'd never had the urge to do it.

Veronica looked good, fantastic, considering she'd had a baby; I could see motherhood had made a change in her. The fact she'd come here, the clothes she was wearing, a white and brown matching Gucci suit, could have been brand new. Either way, she looked good, with new short boob hair. I loved her hair, but she'd cut it. Her choice and it made her look older, but then it could have been the time we'd spent apart and the fact she was now a mother.

"You can hold him if you like?" She came closer and put her hand on my back.

"Wait! How did you find me?"

She said, "Diego."

"Fuck!" Then I covered my mouth thinking about our child's first word being a cuss word. Back in the day, I would have been proud of such a thing, now I felt ashamed of it. I'd seen hard-working people, normal people raise their kids to be good, which meant they had respect not only for their elders but their friends, too. I'd been brought up to think everyone who wasn't in your bloodline was below you and didn't deserve your love, let alone your respect.

"Yes. Do you think he didn't know where you were all this time? Did you think he would let you go and think, great he's gone to lead a good life, I won't have to watch him anymore."

She had a point, and I should have known better than to think Diego would take over and not be worried about my whereabouts. He was acting the same way I would have if I was in charge. He was making sure I didn't come back and if I did, then he would be one step ahead of me. I'd taught him well, maybe a little too well, and I should have been proud of him, but some part of me resented him for it.

"Have you been in Chicago all this time?" I wanted to know more about her life, I didn't know if I was going to see her again, but I took the opportunity to ask her.

"No. In New Jersey. A quiet town. I bought a small house, and we've been fine. I met a couple of moms in a baby group. They've been good, so we're fine. We're doing...okay." She shrugged and part of me wondered if she said the last part for my benefit or for her own.

"So, are you going to hold him or stand there staring at him?" she asked as she studied me as if she wanted to see the monster, the one she'd left behind so many months ago.

I confessed, "I've never held a baby, I'm worried I would hurt him."

She didn't judge or even mock me. If anything, her brows met together as she approached me.

"It's okay. I'll show you how, you don't have to be afraid of him, or me."

I nodded, as I moved and we stood side-by-side, she smelled of fresh roses, the same way she looked too. Whereas I smelt of cold, oil, and fresh winter. We came from completely different worlds, and like before, I didn't know if we could come together, I was even more positive we couldn't right now.

"First things first. Go wash your hands."

I headed to the sink in the corner of my room. I made sure I scrubbed my hands, so no inch or part of it would be dirty. When I was finished, I made sure I didn't use the towel partially filled with oil to dry it. I grabbed some hand towels and admired her as she made baby faces at him, even if he was asleep.

"What's his name?"

"Rik."

"Oh," the idea she named him after me in some way took me back. Rik. I liked it. I was taken aback as I breathed deeply and then decided to give it a try in holding him.

"What do I do with my arms? Like this?"

I'd grasped my hands together with my elbows out. I'd watched others do it, but never taken note, I never thought I would have to until now.

"Watch," she whispered as she moved closer towards him, I knew she was doing it all in slow motion because she wanted me to observe, so I would do the same. Then she put her elbow to the bed and then scooped him up, with her hand into her elbow. I'd seen it done before, they always made sure the head was safe, rather than the rest of the body. She turned to me smiling, and then whispered, "Now, your turn."

I tried to repeat the same thing, but my arms were shaking, I was so fucking nervous, but it didn't deter her from moving him into my arms. She continued to do it, until like her I had him completely in my arms. He was so tired, innocent, and then he yawned and started to wiggle. I laughed at the idea we were once this small, so small and innocent and then over the years, something completely different became of us.

"How old is he?"

"Six weeks. He wanted to come out early. We were in the hospital for three weeks, but then we came out. He was big, even for a small one and he's been growing so much since then. I can't believe he's nearly two months old."

I nodded, as I moved away from her, wanting to see him in the light, the one light in this cabin.

"Neither can I, I thought you would be giving birth any day now."

She laughed. "No, remember when I left, I said I was around six weeks pregnant. Turns out it was more than two months and a bit, so I had the whole date thing mixed up."

"Ah, okay. You've never done this before, so it makes sense."

The lighting in the cabin was a bit dim, but the light in the middle of the room felt as if the sun was shining on him. I wanted to see as much of him as possible, I wanted this moment to last because afterward, who knew what would happen. I didn't want to think about that right now, I wanted to enjoy him.

"I can tell he's going to be like his dad."

I shook my head. "Don't say. I don't want him to be nothing like me. Nothing like me at all."

She smiled as she put her hand on my shoulder.

"Your landlady Monica was telling me all about you, Lucas.

You have been kind, you helped fix the roof when her husband couldn't do it because of his leg. You help so many people around town."

I laughed. "Monica has a big mouth. She doesn't even know who you are."

"I know, but she knew Rik was your son and I'm—"

I moved away from her, not because I didn't want to be close, but I felt like a monster. The one I'd been running away from crawling back inside of me. The monster would have put the baby down and taken her on top of his bed, no questions asked, I didn't want to be that man anymore. So, I created a gap, realizing that after all this time, she still lit up the fire inside of me, the one I thought was truly blown out.

"Who would have thought someone like me, could have a quiet life?"

She shook her head. "I never thought you would, which is why I never believed you being part of Rik's life would be a good idea."

"So, what changed your mind?"

She smiled. "I bumped into Juan and his wife, they were shopping casually, we never spoke, but I watched them. You could say I turned into a stalker that day. I spent all afternoon instead of taking the message and couple of hours Jen gave me as a treat for my birthday, following them."

She sat back on the bed as if she was tired and started to relive the moment.

"Until I saw Juan, I thought it wasn't possible. Seeing Juan with a baby on the way, and another kid in his hand made me think it was possible."

"His wife is pregnant?"

She nodded. "Yeah, you didn't know?"

I shook my head. "I knew he had one kid, but not he was going to have two. I even thought they lived in Italy."

She smiled. "They did, Diego told me, but not anymore.

When I left the house, the day when I last saw you, Diego came to the house and he gave me his card He told me if I needed anything I should call him. So, I did. I must admit I was shocked when he told me you'd disappeared..."

I shrugged, thinking about the irony in her sentence. I hadn't done a good job if all she had to do was call Diego and he gave her an address.

"I tried to and didn't do a good job of it, seeing as you found me so easily. How long before you called him had he given you my address?"

"A day or it could have been two. It was a few weeks ago, I was pregnant and then back then, didn't know what I was going to do with this information. You see, there's still a lot of people who want you to pay for what your dad did to their family, but for some reason, I think Diego keeps them at bay. Especially relatives of Ma."

Shit, Mario and Ma. I forgot about them, made sense that they would seek revenge after Ma not only killed her son, but Jose ended up killing her, too. They didn't want anything leading back to us, more importantly, me.

"He told you this?"

I was shocked Diego was going out of his way to protect me. Some part of me felt proud I'd taught him how to have some morals, but then the other part knew he was now in charge of what I'd left behind and there was nothing to be proud of.

"No. But it is the only thing which makes sense."

I couldn't keep on like this. I was getting too comfortable with the little one in my arms and her being in my cabin.

"Why did you come Veronica? Why are you here?"

I handed Rik back to her, and then moved away, and she seemed shocked by the change in my tone.

"Don't you want us here? Aren't you happy to meet him?" she asked.

"It's not about what I want or what I need, it's about why did you come?"

She sighed. "I don't know. Did I come to tell you to forget the past and let's move forward? No. Did I come to tell you Rik and I were moving to Alaska, no. I know I haven't been able to get you out of mind, and when I thought that there was a chance, you would be like....well...like this, I had to come and see for myself."

"I see. I think the little one is probably tired and there's a hotel, so maybe it's better if you stay there for the night."

A tear escaped, and I avoided eye contact because I knew I had nothing to offer them. She was right. The only option would be for them to come and live with me here, which wasn't an option. What would we do together, hurl snow?

"Right. We better get going, he'll need a feeding soon."

With haste, she took the car chair in the corner of the room, strapped him in. Kissed his forehead, put on her jacket and like that, she was ready to go.

"My keys," she said as she passed me to get to the table. We froze, standing staring at each other, she was waiting for me to make a move and I didn't want to make her stay. My heart was crying at the idea of them walking out of the door and never seeing them again. I smelled him, held him in my arms, and was ready to give it up. She said she came, and didn't know the reasons why, it was a lie. She came, for what I was about to do.

I held her in my arms, and then I swept her up, waiting for her permission to do so much more, she did nothing but gasp, and slowly open her mouth and hold back her head.

I slowly met her lips, I kissed on top of it, to the side and the bottom of each. Each time, she held it lightly open, waiting for my tongue to enter her mouth. I did at first, as her breathing started to become heavy, and once I kissed her, I made sure that I had no intention of letting her go, the monster the man I used to be once returned and claimed her.

I loved her. There was no turning back from the feelings I had for her. She felt the same way, too. She didn't just come to introduce me to our son, she came here to be with me. Love brought her to me and I was never going to shove her away again. She and our son was home and I cherished both of them. Love had saved me and given me a family.

EPILOGUE

eronica

WE HAVE BEEN LIVING as a family in Alaska since the day I came to the cabin. I couldn't deny this was my reason for coming here, to be with the man I loved, the father of my child. The man was a monster, but now had provided us with a loving home in the woods.

We built a house from scratch. Who would have thought this small town girl, turned city girl would love living in the wilderness. It was as if I'd found my inner peace by living here.

Ricardo cut contact with Juan while wishing him well. It was time to say goodbye to his old life and focus on his new one. I did take a little money out of the pot, not only to build the house but to work on my online business. I promised one day I would give it all to charity, in the meantime, while my PA business takes off, I'm still trying to get it off the ground, but it's a little difficult with one kid and another on its way.

"You shouldn't be lifting," Ricardo said as I brought in some logs from outside and attempted to build a fire.

"It's cold and stop fussing. There's nothing wrong with me carrying a few logs. Besides, shouldn't you be at work?"

"Don't remind me. It seems every year the winter gets worse and more roads to get blocked."

I smiled, kissing him on the cheek as he took the logs out of my hands. "This is why you need an assistant."

He said, "Yeah, but I make barely enough for us, let alone paying someone."

I wasn't going to mention it, as we'd argued about it more than once, but he could get his hands on money if he wanted to. He could ask Diego or even Juan for a loan, but he refused to do it. My husband was not only stubborn, but he was proud, too. It was weird, to get married and be surrounded by our new family, the one we'd created in this small town. The ones who seemed to love us, the way we were now, compared to what we used to be.

"I have exactly twenty minutes to do as much around this house as possible, before I have to go and pick up Rik."

He shook his head. "I'll do it. Besides, he loves riding at the back of the truck. You can get on with whatever you have to do, including cooking my Lourde's paella recipe."

I nodded, "Fine, I gather you want it tonight. Even though it'll take me all afternoon to finish preparing it."

He smiled, as he kissed me on the cheek. This meant I had to spend most of my time cooking, rather than spending time on social media, which at times was a good thing and not a bad thing. I had a couple of clients, and I had completed most of their work this morning. Now, I had to try and get at least three more clients so I could break even and start earning some real money. I told myself I had to be patient. Sometimes it was all about word of mouth.

As for Jen, my one true friend, once she was married, they

had a honeymoon baby and with the move, we'd lost touch. She became busy with her new mom's group and I was busy building a house and a life here. We keep in touch, but we know we'll most likely never meet again. It is for the best. We could never be in each other's lives, not like we before.

"Remember not to get distracted and be home on time."

He winked, "As if I would dream of being late, knowing there will be a paella on the table."

I laughed, as I thought about the man who used to have a perfect physique looking as if he was expecting a baby too. Only one of us was pregnant in this house.

Life is what you make it, and it may be cold in Nome, but this house is full of love. The past is something we don't talk about, but I know at times that Ricardo's nightmares will come back to haunt him; like the anniversary of his dad's death or even his birthday. Those are the times when Ricardo goes dark and he remembers the past. It still haunts him, but I'm hoping in time the cobwebs will eventually fade away and we will be happy always. I love Ricardo and our life together. I know one thing for sure, I couldn't ask for more, and neither could he.

ABOUT THE AUTHOR

P. A. Thomas is an emerging author of thrillers. This is P. A.'s first book.

Printed in Great Britain
by Amazon